Praises for Isabel's Gifts

A sweet story of a child's Christmas, of poverty and riches, of sacrifice and miracles, and of timeless spiritual truths.

—Paul Robertson, author of *The Heir,* (Bethany House)

If one accepts and uses the gifts Isabel's story offers, one will learn what Isabel's mother meant when she said, 'The person who gives and the person who receives get the same gift.' One may come to understand how the gift of a child–given and received so long ago–received and given again by hearts like Isabel's will save the world. A touching re–telling of the *The* Christmas story.

—Jean Denton, Writer and Catholic reporter

In the honored tradition of Dickens' *A Christmas Carol*—this time through the eyes of a young girl—Dr. Silva–Barbeau offers an endearing parable of life as God has intended for all of us to live: humbly and graciously in service to others. May Isabel's Gift bless all who read it.

—Kimberly Iverson, author of *Liberty* (HQN)

Dr. Silva–Barbeau tells a story and she tells it from experience and with imagination, warmth and deep faith. Best of all, she tells her story from the heart.

—John Omwake, author of *Neola's Run* and
Songs for Aging Children.

Using her rich childhood experiences from the Cape Verde Islands, Irma Silva–Barbeau blends her story of gift giving through the customs and traditions of the local people and their deep religious faith. Isabel's journey of self–exploration focuses on the universal traits of love and compassion for the fellow human being, thus transcending the boundaries of religions. The little Catholic girl speaks to all who want to hear her message that both the receiver and the giver are enriched by the power of the same gift. What a wonderful lesson for all of us!

—Mary H. Jakubowski, author of *Whispers from the Steppe*

October 1, 2008

ISABEL'S
GIFT

*To Darlene, a fellow
writer-author, with
best wishes.*

[signature]

ISABEL'S
GIFT

A Story of Giving, Love, and Discovery

Irma Silva-Barbeau, Ph.D.
Author of *A Sweet Oblation*

TATE PUBLISHING & *Enterprises*

Published by Tate Publishing & Enterprises, LLC
127 E. Trade Center Terrace | Mustang, Oklahoma 73064 USA
1.888.361.9473 | www.tatepublishing.com

Tate Publishing is committed to excellence in the publishing industry. The company reflects the philosophy established by the founders, based on Psalm 68:11,
"The Lord gave the word and great was the company of those who published it."

Book design copyright © 2007 by Tate Publishing, LLC. All rights reserved.
Cover design by Jacob Crissup
Interior design by Lindsay B. Behrens

Published in the United States of America

ISBN: 978–1–60462–150–1
1. Christian Fiction   2. YAL   3. Christmas
07.12.06

Dedication

In memory of my mother,
Maria José dos Santos e Silva (Djédjé)

Acknowledgments

I have discovered that writing and publishing a book is often a collaborative effort between the writer and her group of friends. I have been blessed with such group of friends. I am deeply grateful for all my friends who read the different drafts of this book and made constructive comments and gave me encouragement.

I am especially indebted to Catherine Merola who spent so much time with me going over the manuscript that she should be on the payroll.

A warm thank you goes to my proof readers and wonderful commentators, Emily Crawford, Mona Charney, Rachel Garrity, Kimberly Iverson, and John Stabbs.

I am also grateful to Drs. T. Charles Pfaff and Virginia Burggraf for their reading and encouragement.

A special thank you goes to Tate Publishing for believing in my book and publishing it.

I thank my family for their undying support.

Finally, I thank God, His angels, and saints for my life, family, friends and inspiration to write.

Contents

Foreword

As the harvest time on the Cape Verde Islands merges with Advent in a season of hope, Isabel's family struggles yet another year to manage on the uneven yield of the land. Isabel listens to her faith–filled mother's words of gratitude for God's providence and tries to get her nine–year–old mind around how their simple gifts and celebration of the baby Jesus' birthday can possibly compare to the ornate Christmas tree and lavish stack of presents pictured on a postcard from her aunt in America.

But surprising new pangs of confusion arise as she fixes her heart's desire on a pair of fine leather shoes and calls her wish toward the sky each day in anticipation of *Nhō Bedjo*, Santa's Christmas Eve visit.

From the moving portrayal of her revelation as she gazes upon the poor bare feet of her little friends, we are carried, through the eyes and fertile imagination of young Isabel, on a disquieting night's journey of enlightenment.

In *Isabel's Gift: A Story of Giving, Love and Discovery*, her second novel, Irma Silva–Barbeau again draws on her rich childhood experience of life and the religious tradition of the island of Brava, the Cape Verde Islands off the coast of Senegal. If one accepts and uses the gifts Isabel's story offers, one will learn what Isabel's mother meant when she said, "The person who gives and the person who receives get the same gift." And one may come to understand how the gift of a child—given and received so long ago—received and given again by hearts like Isabel's will save the world. A touching re–telling of *the* Christmas story.

Jean Denton, Writer and Catholic Reporter

...It is more blessed to give than to receive.

Acts 20:35

It is the intention behind your giving and receiving that is the most important thing. The intention should always be to create happiness for the giver and receiver, because happiness is life–supporting and life–sustaining and therefore generates increase. The return is directly proportional to the giving when it is unconditional and from the heart.

The Seven Spiritual Laws of Success: A Practical
Guide to the Fulfillment of Your Dreams by
Deepak Chopra

Preface

I began writing in a period of my life when I realized that, for most of my adult life, what I had been working for so forcefully, so diligently, and with such a passion and dedication no longer seemed to produce the fruits that I had hoped. My soul was thirsty. My soul was hungry, and no matter how hard I worked, and how long I persisted, I remained in poverty—hungering, thirsting and lost in the byways of life.

I began to write essays reflecting on my life experiences, professional experiences, family life and childhood. This period also coincided with my elderly parents' failing health and eventual death. It was a period of immeasurable loss for me. I lost my parents, and I lost the direction in my career. In addition, health problems within my own immediate family exacerbated this feeling of loss.

I had read once that life was not supposed to be this hard and if it was hard, it was because one was trying to run on the wrong tracks. Stop! Reflect! Change tracks! And so I did.

I began to search. I read, discussed and argued. I joined book groups, and I started one of my own to explore other philosophies and other religious traditions. I began to accept everything. If I were reading a book about Hinduism, it made perfect sense to me. If I read a book on New Age or Buddhism for example, they all made perfect sense to me. They made sense because they all have some element of truth that resonated with me, but I could not embrace any one of them because they all left me still wanting.

This process in my search continued for a few years, until one day, while I was on vacation at the beach in North Carolina I saw a sign for a discounted bookstore. I went in and I went straight to the book *Blessed Art Thou Among Women: Reflections on Mary in Our World Today*.[1] It was a book written about our Blessed Mother Mary by the staff of *Life* Magazine. The book was a series of synopses on what Mary meant to different people.

At that same time, St. Mary's Catholic Church in Blacksburg, Virginia, had a book discussion group and the group leader, one day after Mass, approached me and asked me if I would like to join the group. They were planning to read *The Cloister Walk*[2] by Kathleen Norris. This book introduced me to the concept of *lectio divina,* a slow meditative spiritual reading. This was my first introduction to reading with the heart.

Kathleen Norris, an oblate of the Benedictine Order, also in this book introduced me to the *Rule of St. Benedict*[3] which among other things encourages listening with the "ear of the heart."

"And Mary kept all these things, reflecting on them in her heart" (Luke 2:19). Mary, the Mother of Jesus, lived her life with the heart. She was quiet, not boastful of being the mother of the wonder child, intuitive and intelligent boy, the spiritual man, the son of God. She became His first disciple. She did not completely understand what God was asking of her, but she stepped onto the stones of the path of life with complete awe, wonder, hope, and with faith.

It doesn't matter where one lives—in The Cape Verde Islands where this book takes place or in New York City; in Međugorje or in Salt Lake City; in Djakarta or in Paris— we all live, irrespective of our social status, not completely understanding, the *whys*, the *whats*, the *whens*, the *hows*, and the *wheres* of our lives.

I do believe that Mary, the Mother of Jesus, came to my life when my soul was dark and heavy, and she pointed me, as she had done to the stewards at the marriage at Cana, to do as her Son says. She also brought to my life great women of faith, such as *St. Thérèse of Lisieux, St. Theresa of Avila* and *St. Maria Faustina Kowalska* as examples of how to "live with the heart" and how they kept Jesus in the center of their lives.

Isabel's Gift, as with my previous book, *A Sweet Oblation*, and *The Feasts*, which is forthcoming, although written in a fictionalized storyline presents, in most parts, real events that occurred either in my own family as I grew up, or events that occurred in my adult life and my personal reflections on these events.

My writing, therefore, is a reflection on "living with a heart," that is, acknowledging that nothing happens by "chance," that we are given choices to live the kind of life that we choose, and at every junction we are given direction and options. All we need to do is be willing to listen, read, and pray with the heart.

It is my hope that all those who read this book, be they Catholics or Protestants, Muslims or Jews, Buddhists or Hindus, New Age or atheists, will recognize something of themselves in the young protagonist, Isabel, which will contribute to a greater understanding of the world in which we live and how we are all related.

The Altar

...there is no true happiness in owning and taking but only in giving.

Wisdom from the Monastery. A program of
Spiritual Healing edited by Peter Sewald

Isabel Rodrigues was lying down with her belly flat on the wooden floor, knees bent and legs sticking up in the air exposing the dirty soles of her bare feet. While keeping her mother company, Isabel had drifted off into her own little world intently watching a spider reel in a catch for its dinner.

It was a quiet peaceful afternoon on the first of December. Mrs. Rodrigues was standing by the window facing the livestock courtyard of their family home. Just beyond the walls separating the courtyard from the fields, she could see the papaya and banana trees, laden with fruit, and the lower branches of the coffee and the orange trees touching the ground under the weight of their abundance. She closed her eyes and took a deep breath, and in that breath a little prayer of thanksgiving bubbled up and tears trickled down her cheeks. She brought the palms of her hands up, and covered her mouth. She breathed in deeply again, catching her breath; she stood still for a little while, charmed by the gentle whistle of the easterly winds and the birds' serenade to the setting sun.

She opened her eyes and looked out the window, and her heart leaped with joy as she saw the family mule and two donkeys coming in loaded with the last of the corn crop from their fields in the highlands of Cachás. The harvest had been better than they had expected thanks to the good steady rains in the higher altitudes. The irrigated crops in Ferrero looked promising too. In spite of the late rains, the springs had been replenished ensuring the success of the irrigated vegetables, fruit trees, and sugar cane.

At home, their underground cistern was almost full of rainwater. Mrs. Rodrigues gave a loud sigh of relief, saying to herself, *This year we will be all right, and perhaps there will be something left for Raymond and me to indulge the children a little this Christmas.* The previous harvests had been so meager that it had been hard for them to scrape up anything to celebrate the holiday.

A donkey bray brought her back to the task at hand, and she began quickly to fill with soil the twelve empty cups, which were standing on a row on top of the windowsill in front of her. She carefully sowed as many yellow kernels of corn in each one as possible. Then she tenderly began to water them as she said thoughtfully, "Hopefully in twenty–two days these corn seedlings will look full and green for our altar."

"What did you say, Mother?" replied Isabel, looking up from the floor.

"I was just saying that I hope that this *siera*—the greenery for our Christmas altar will be ready. Christmas will be here in less than a month," Mrs. Rodrigues reminded Isabel, looking down at her.

"Really!" said Isabel, abandoning the spider and rising quickly to her feet. "I wish that we could have a Christmas tree just like the one in the postcard that Auntie sent us from America." Mrs. Rodrigues' only sister, Mana, lived in California and very conscientiously sent her younger sister, Margaret, and her family packages of goods at every opportunity. This year she had also sent a beautiful Christmas card depicting a huge Christmas tree that was fully trimmed. All around the base of the tree were beautiful brightly colored packages, and at the far corner of the card there were two children peeking at the tree from behind a doorway. Isabel had become enchanted with the tree and fantasized about what kind of gifts would be inside the boxes. She often imagined herself inside the card itself peeking from behind the doorway with the other children.

"Well, that would be nice, but we don't have trees like that around here, and even if we did, what would we put on a tree?" Mrs. Rodrigues said matter-of-factly.

"Well, why can't we then, at least, put our presents at the foot of the altar just like they put their presents at the foot of the tree? That would be better than just an altar with green corn seedlings and oranges, and grown up boots next to the bed for presents," Isabel said, and continued rather disgruntled, "Why, if I were to make a postcard of our Christmas and send it to a little girl like me where Auntie lives, she would not think it was much fun at all." Isabel emphasized "*at all*."

Mrs. Rodrigues was used to Isabel's questioning and her endless fantasies about the world outside the island. She bent down and looked straight into Isabel's big hazel eyes, and with a smile said, "Oh, I don't know about that. In fact, it is pretty interesting the way we do things around here. Do you know why we make an altar for Christmas?"

"No," Isabel responded, shaking her head.

"Come here. I want to show you something," her mother said. Taking Isabel's hand, Mrs. Rodrigues went into her own room. In a corner of the room there was a wardrobe, and on top of the wardrobe there was a statue of Jesus as a child about four or five-years-old. The statue wore a cream-colored satin gown with lacy trim and was protected by a glass dome.

"You see that statue of the child Jesus?" Mrs. Rodrigues asked, pointing to the top of the wardrobe. "This is the statue that we always put on top of our Christmas altar. It came from America, where Auntie lives. My mother found it in a house that they were renting in New Bedford, in America. When she came back home to the Cape Verde Islands, she brought it with her. Ever since I can remember, this statue has always been here."

"But why is he wearing a dress?" Isabel asked.

"I don't know," Mrs. Rodrigues answered simply, and continued, "It was my grandmother who began the tradition of making an altar for Christmas. She brought the custom from the island of Madeira, where she grew up. The altar is something like a Christmas tree. You see how it is wide at the bottom?" As she took four wooden square boxes from the back of the wardrobe and began to pile the boxes up one on top of the other, Mrs. Rodrigues explained, "We put this medium–sized box on top of the big box, then this smaller one on top of that one, and then this smallest on top of them all. Here at the top is where we put the statue of the child Jesus."

Isabel listened carefully as her mother demonstrated how the altar was put together. "You see, it is like stairs to heaven," continued Mrs. Rodrigues. "We are at the bottom and Jesus is in heaven at the top. To get to Jesus we have to climb up the stairs."

"Hmm," murmured Isabel.

"This statue has brought many blessings to our family throughout the years, and we make an altar as a way to celebrate Jesus' birthday."

"Why do we use the corn seedlings?" Isabel asked.

"Well, here where we live is normally a very dry place, so we want to put something pretty and fresh on the altar. The greenery is for life, for things that grow here on earth. It is like an offering, a gift from our land, and besides, it makes the altar look pretty," she explained.

"What about the oranges?" Isabel asked.

"Well," Mrs. Rodrigues laughed. "You know about the orange trees in the backyard?"

Isabel nodded her head and said, "There are several with fruit almost ready to eat.

"That is right," said Mrs. Rodrigues. "Soon it will be the season for oranges. We are blessed to have so many trees and so many delicious oranges. So, I began to put them on the altar because their bright color made the altar come alive. I guess it is also my way of thanking Jesus for all that we have, and besides, when guests come to wish us Merry Christmas, they always leave with fresh oranges. Not everybody has oranges like we do."

"Oh!" Isabel exclaimed.

"So what do you think, Isabel? Do you think that a little girl from where Auntie lives would find the way we celebrate Christmas interesting?" she asked.

"I guess, but they get presents, many presents!" Isabel reminded her mother.

"We get presents, too. When we set up our altar in our house it is like inviting Jesus to come live with us for a little while and to celebrate His birthday. When Jesus is our guest, when He is in our home and in our hearts, many, many, wonderful things happen," she said.

"Like what?" Isabel asked.

"We get gifts, great gifts! Christmas Eve is a magical night when we can get many things, if we ask in the right way, and *if* we also give," said her mother.

Isabel frowned saying, "What do you mean, Mother?"

"Giving and receiving are the same things, you know. Presents can be anything that comes from the heart and makes both the person who receives and the one who gives feel good and happy."

"I don't understand," said Isabel, rather confused.

Mrs. Rodrigues sat at the edge of her bed with Isabel next to her and said, "You like to keep me company when I am working alone, like right now?" Isabel nodded. "I like it when you keep me company instead of being outside playing with your friends," she said, then added, "When you keep me company like this, I feel loved. I feel happy, and I love you for…"

Isabel quickly interrupted, "I keep you company because I don't want you to be all by yourself, because I love you, and I want you to be happy!"

"That is right, Isabel. So we both get the same thing. We both get happiness. That is why giving and receiving are the same things. It doesn't matter if the gift is keeping someone company or giving someone a kiss or offering someone a flower. The person who gives and the person who receives get the same gift of happiness," explained Mrs. Rodrigues finally.

"Interesting!" replied Isabel, not quite convinced.

Her mother smiled and patted her head. They sat quietly for a few minutes each deep in thought. Then, a loud voice erupted up from the kitchen courtyard calling Isabel's name. "Isabel! Isabel! Time to wash up!"

Isabel frowned, and her mother said, "Go. You got yourself pretty dirty today. My goodness, look at those feet. Scrub them well and don't give Maria any trouble." Maria was the family's live–in helper.

Isabel reluctantly began to walk toward the stairs, then hesitated as though with a question, but her mother waved her away. Mrs. Rodrigues went back to her newly seeded cups, storing them away for the night. She listened as Isabel's bare feet shuffled their way down the wooden stairs. Then she heard Isabel's feisty voice arguing with Maria about how cold the water was and how extensively she had to wash up. Mrs. Rodrigues smiled and shook her head slightly as she pondered on the grumblings of her nine– year–old.

The Shoes

For where your treasure is, there also will your heart be.

Luke 12:34

Mrs. Rodrigues' story of giving and receiving made a deep impression on Isabel, especially the part about asking and getting what you want. So, she decided that this Christmas she was going to ask for a pair of beautiful shoes that she had seen in a magazine at her friend Dee's house. The shoes were white with small garlands of flowers stamped out in the leather all around the borders. Each shoe had a wide strap that buckled on the side. Dee said that it was in the highest fashion in Lisbon, where she had just been visiting her sister. Isabel imagined herself looking dashing in those shoes, the envy of all her friends as they played in the park on Christmas afternoon.

Now, as it happened, shoes for children, although highly desired, were not a priority on the island. Not because the people did not consider them important, but because there was no money to buy them. Theirs was a family farming society where you ate what you grew, and there was very little left to sell. The major source of cash for the Rodrigues was their *grogo*—a precious sugar cane rum, from their irri-gated land in Ferrero. But more often than not, they used the *grogo* to barter for other goods and services. The first prior-ity was food, then clothes, then medicine, and then school notebooks. The few children who wore shoes all the time during the week were the sons and daughters of the most successful merchants, or those whose fathers worked abroad and sent remittances, or those who were from families of the higher echelon civil servants. (You always knew who those families were: they were the ones who had a running tab at the local stores and were valued by the merchants as their top customers because they had a steady check coming in every month.)

So even though the Rodrigues family were prominent members of their community, their younger children went barefoot during the week. They had for each child a pair of sandals or some other type of footwear just for Sundays to go to Mass, or for visits to relatives, or for Sunday walks in the park. Otherwise, you washed your feet before you went to school or ran errands. When the Rodrigues chil-dren turned thirteen, they were considered young men and young women, who should not be seen barefoot, at least in public. So their parents had whatever footwear was available recycled or resoled by the local shoemaker, thereby keeping him in business, because the making of a brand new pair of shoes was a very rare event.

Isabel, however, was not aware of any of this. Although she went barefoot everywhere, as her friends did, she did have her one pair of sandals, hand–me–downs from her sis-ter Fern, which were constantly being polished and re–polished whenever she had to go someplace special. Only one of her friends, Dee, wore shoes all the time. But Dee was not from Brava. Dee came from the island of São Vicente, and her father was the nurse and sometimes the doctor for the island, since doctors never seemed to stay for long. And besides, Dee was considered foreign. Foreign people had a special status. They always wore shoes and Isabel never thought beyond that. It never occurred to Isabel that the reason that she and her two younger sisters, Ida and Mandy, went barefoot was because her parents couldn't afford shoes. She thought it was not their custom, and that she would get her shoes whenever she came of age, like her two older sisters, Eliza and Fern. She had felt perfectly comfortable with that until one day just last September, when her friend Dee had arrived from spending her summer vacation in Lisbon.

September was a traumatic and emotional month for many families in the island. It was the month when many would say goodbye to their young boys who were enrolled in high school on the islands of São Vicente and Santiago. Isabel's two older brothers, Andy and Joseph, were among this group of boys who would arrive home in June after the exams and would leave in late September to begin classes on October first. Dee was the exception; she was the only child coming to Brava for school. She and Isabel were both in the same grade, but Dee's knowledge of the outside world was way beyond Isabel's. Just in the area of food, for instance, Dee had eaten apples, cherries, and grapes, and had drunk "sodas," a drink that was so rare that the children had only heard stories of it.

Dee had also taken tea in Lisbon's most renowned tea-rooms. She had indulged often in the Portuguese's tastiest of confections—ice cream, which, despite Dee's elaborate explanations, Isabel could not fathom in her mind what it was like. Something that cold?

Nobody in Brava had ever had ice cream because no one, with exception of the medical doctor, had a refrigerator. Once, one of the doctor's children brought a piece of ice to the park and Isabel got a chance to hold it and lick it. It was the strangest and most delightful thing that Isabel had ever experienced. Dee kept saying, "Ice cream is like the ice, but it is creamy like butter and tastes like cake." Dee would describe all these things to Isabel during their little walks in the park. Isabel would listen closely, filled with admiration.

Isabel always had a hard time in the summer or whenever Dee was away. Dee was her best, best friend. She would miss her terribly and always waited with great anticipation for her friend to return.

It was a Wednesday afternoon, this September day, and Isabel was sitting on the bench in front of her house playing with her sisters. Ida was two years younger than she, and Mandy, who was the youngest in the family, was just about five years younger than Isabel. Earlier that day, they had heard the news that a ship from São Vicente had arrived. Isabel never knew exactly when Dee would arrive; usually she would just show up at their house.

That day a friend of Eliza's, who lived near Dee's house, came by with the news: Dee and her family had indeed arrived. "You should see Dee. She is tall now, and her skin is as smooth as satin. Well, she is a young woman, she looks like she is thirteen!" Isabel wilted with the news; it appeared that Dee was now everything that she was not. Dee was tall and could be taken for thirteen while Isabel was short and often was mistaken for being six. Isabel feared that she had lost her best friend.

The next day, Isabel carefully got ready to meet her friend. She scrubbed up and put on the best dress that she was allowed for a weekday. She would have put on her Sunday sandals but her mother would not have allowed it for play on a casual Thursday afternoon in the park. Isabel wanted to add a little bit of sophistication of her own, so she took one of her mother's kerchiefs, white with large red roses, and draped it over her head securing it with a knot just below her chin, just like Dee used to do when she went out in the evenings. She tried to dash out of the house without being seen, but Fern got a glimpse of her and yelled out, "Hey Isabel, what is up with the kerchief?"

Isabel pretended that she had not heard and began to walk faster towards the park, but Ida immediately chimed in, "She is going to meet Dee!"

"Oh," was all that Fern could say. She felt sorry for Isabel. All the Rodrigues girls were anticipating the meeting with Dee, since from what their friend had reported, Dee had been completely transformed over the summer. But Isabel looked completely ridiculous with her calico sleeveless dress and bare feet, with the oversized kerchief in full bloom on her head. Fern caught up to her and took the kerchief off her head, saying, "You don't need that, Isabel. Your hair is too pretty to cover up."

As Isabel was to find out, Dee was indeed almost as tall as Fern and was rivaling Fern in beauty, but, in spite of those external changes, their friendship had not changed. Dee was still one in soul with her, except—Dee now was not just wearing shoes; she was wearing fine white leather shoes from Lisbon. And that began to stir some uncomfortable feelings in Isabel. She did not understand those feelings. These were new feelings that caused her heart to ache. Isabel did not like these feelings. She was convinced that it had to do with the shoes and that if she had those same shoes those feelings would go away.

So, Christmas and her mother's story presented a clear opportunity for Isabel to get the long desired shoes. *Didn't Mother say that you could get whatever you asked for?* she reasoned. She told her sisters about the shoes and she had Dee cut out the picture of the shoes from the magazine. She showed her mother the picture. She showed her father the picture. Everyone agreed that this was a fine pair of shoes, and that indeed Isabel would look great with them. But Mrs. Rodrigues cautioned, "Isabel, you know that gifts at Christmas do not come from us," as she looked at her husband, Raymond.

"Yes, I know that. It comes from the *Nhō Bedjo*, Santa," she replied, pointing toward the sky.

"Well, don't count on it, Isabel," Eliza interjected. "Santa has been pretty poor these past Christmases. Fern got only two pieces of candy in her boot last year, and she was so mad that she threw them right out of the window. Not that I blamed her for feeling that way. I found the candy and ate them."

"Well, this Christmas is going to be different," Isabel responded confidently.

In God's Hands

Happy those whose trust is the Lord.

Psalms 40.5

In spite of past disappointments during Christmas, the young Rodrigueses were overly optimistic this year. With most of the crops in from the fields, Mr. Rodrigues had stopped holding his breath. He was feeling the same relief that his wife was feeling, *This year we are going to be all right!*

They lived from cropping season to cropping season, and everyone in the family was acquainted with the many hardships that Mr. and Mrs. Rodrigues, and their ancestors in general, had lived through. Often after a particularly good dinner, Mr. Rodrigues would keep his children riveted by his many stories of poor rainfall and failed crops.

"In the olden days," Mr. Rodrigues recalled, "water wars were common," referring to the rains.

"Water wars—you mean water fights like those of Fern and Joseph?" Ida asked, furrowing her brow.

"No, water wars—of grown ups with rifles. People are civilized now, but in the days of my grandfather when it rained, they used to go out in their tall rubber boots and dig canals on the ground and try to divert all the water running off the side of the mountains into their underground cisterns and into their own lands. I will never forget this. I must have been your age, Isabel. It was late in June. I remember it clearly because it was the day after the feast of St. John the Baptist. My grandfather and his brother never got along. They were always mad at each other about this and that. Well, that year we had had very little rain and on that day we had one of those torrential rains. I guess all the prayers to St. John the Baptist paid off, because it appeared that all the rains for that year were falling on that one single day. So, my grandfather went out with his shovel and began to divert the water to his property. No sooner did he do that, than his brother came out with his own shovel and half a dozen of his workers doing the same thing—diverting water to his own property. Soon, my grandfather called out some of his workers, and they continued to divert the water toward my grandfather's property. Then his brother went inside the house and got a rifle. My grandfather did the same. They first began to exchange some mean words and then they began to fire shots in the air, and they continued with this for several rounds of firing up in the air, until my grandmother came out and stood between them and put a stop to it before anyone got hurt. My grandfather and his brother did not speak to each other for a long time. My brother and I were forbidden to go up the street and visit our granduncle and cousins."

"Did they ever make up?" Eliza asked.

"I am not sure. I hope so. Imagine going to your grave mad because of the rains," Mr. Rodrigues said.

"Rain comes from heaven. It belongs to everybody," little Mandy exclaimed.

Everyone turned in amazement toward Mandy. Mr. Rodrigues picked her up and kissed her and said, "That is really true, Mandy. Who told you that?"

"No one. When it rains we all go out and run in the streets playing in it. It belongs to everybody," she answered. The five–year–old had understood this from the custom of having little children run around nude in the rain to welcome it. This past season had been Mandy's first year that she was allowed to strip and join the other "rain children" running around all over the neighborhood playing.

During the months of November and December, even when the harvest was meager, there would be some food available for everyone, and after that, what would come is in the hands of God—*sta na mon de Deus*. Their world had not changed much since their Portuguese ancestors had settled in the island several centuries ago. They had to cope year after year with sporadic rains, droughts and poor harvests that they had developed the attitude of complete dependence on God. They always did all they could, but in the end their future and their survival rested in the hands of God.

Indeed, this reality was always present in the people's minds and was no less so in the minds of Raymond and Margaret Rodrigues. It was almost at the end of World War II, only a decade ago, that they had been able to save their families and others from dying of hunger by the grace of

God. Both had their unique stories of that famine which they had passed down to their children, so that even in the best of times they could remember and give thanks to God. They told their stories often with tears in their eyes.

Mrs. Rodrigues told the story that one day she had gone to the kitchen to find a man dressed in rags, with long hair and a beard, eyes bulging out of their sockets, sagging wrinkled skin draped over his bony skull. He looked like a wild beast in a feeding frenzy. He had both his hands in a bucket in which she saved dishwater, vegetable peels, and other residue from processing corn for the pigs. She was startled, and the man seeing her yelled out, "I am hungry!" as he continued to stuff his mouth with the pigs' slop. Mrs. Rodrigues immediately backed away in fear saying to him, "Eat up, mister! Eat up, mister! Mister, eat it all up! *Nhô comé! Nhô comé! Nhô comé fêpu,*" and she ran back to the main house. That man survived and hung around their house and afterwards became practically a member of their family.

Mr. Rodrigues' story was equally poignant. At that time, he had had a small store in one of the rooms in their house. The government officials made frequent rounds to all such stores on the island to check on their supplies so that they could be redistributed to the population. He kept hidden a fifty-liter drum of corn for his own family. When all the other food had run out, he called all members of his family, including his widowed sister, to come to the house. He brought out the drum and he told them that was absolutely the last bit of food that they had left. He solemnly opened the drum and measured a liter of corn and gave it to his wife. She ground the corn fine and made a thin gruel with water and salt and distributed it in cups to all members. A liter of corn a day saved them from dying of hunger, and when the drum was practically empty, news came that a ship had just docked with food supplies. Mr. Rodrigues could never tell this story without choking in tears and giving thanks to God.

Famines like these were rare, but shortages of food were still common especially for those with little land and with no steady job. When the harvest was poor, by March and April people would begin to tighten their belts.

This year All Saints' Day, on November first, which is the beginning of the harvest season, was celebrated well. Eliza and Fern met with their friends and had a traditional *merenda*—a picnic type lunch, made up with the first fruits of the harvest. It was a meal of fresh corn, and of fresh vegetables and tubers cooked with prime pieces of salted corn. There were also fresh fruits and homemade sweets with lemonade or orangeade. Isabel, Ida and Mandy met up with other children in the neighborhood and had their *merenda* at the house of Nhā Beta. Nhā Beta was a great neighbor of theirs, and she and her two daughters delighted in having the children often at their house for a *merenda* throughout the year, but especially on this day.

This was a time for thanksgiving; thanksgiving for whatever rains had come, for whatever kind of harvest had been, for surviving one more year. Thus they celebrated as they waited and prepared for the coming of Christmas.

The preparation of the *siera* signaled that Christmas was imminent and that they had entered the period of Advent— the Church's time of hope, of preparation and of waiting for the coming of God to earth. It was also a time for charity. The local church would rally the population and collect whatever they could from those with a better harvest to distribute in packages to the poor and the needy throughout the island. The Italian Capuchin fathers were adamant in this and they made a point that no one at Christmas should go hungry and no child empty– handed. Eliza and Fern had been recruited to join the priests,and other young ladies in the town, to walk to the most remote areas of the island distributing one–kilogram packages of sugar, flour, and other goods to the poor.

So the Rodrigues family began to prepare for the *Boas Festas,* the holiday season that begins with Christmas and ends with the Feast of the Kings on January the sixth. This meant ordering in advance butter from the herders' wives, and eggs from anyone who had chickens. Also they had to start buying and stashing away, here and there, sugar and flour, vanilla, baking powder, chocolate and anything else that was needed to make a chocolate marbled cake, a cake of three colors, and the traditional sand cookies. Cake pans were sometimes also borrowed. Few people had them, especially if you wanted to make a heart–shaped cake or a horseshoe shape that were the favorites. You also had to *palabra*—put your name on the baker's list that he kept in his head, to allow you to have a turn at a corner of the hot brick oven that was used for the bread baking.

Mrs. Rodrigues also made *licor,* a sweet drink colored with green or red food coloring and made of diluted *grogo.* This drink was especially for the ladies who, although they drank the hard liquor straight up privately, in public were allowed only the *licor* and should and would politely decline the hard liquor if any unschooled person dared to offer it to them.

Celebration was in the air and nothing, not even the worst harvest, could dampen the spirit of hope, the spirit of charity and joy that overtook this tiny island during this time period of renewal and of all the hopes that come with the New Year.

Preparations

....Prepare the way of the Lord...

Matthew 3:3

The couple of weeks before Christmas were the busiest time in the Rodrigues' household, with all the final preparations for the holidays. Mrs. Rodrigues gave the statue of the child Jesus a bath. She washed and ironed his gown. She was also busy sewing a long, white, crepe dress for Isabel to wear on Christmas Eve. Isabel and several of her friends were going to be little angels standing guard by the crèche of baby Jesus during the Christmas Eve midnight Mass. Women from the church were making small papier–mâché wings and garlands of wax white flowers for the girls' hair.

Everyone helped prepare for the coming of Christmas. Fern kept a close eye on the cups with the corn seedlings, and selected the brightest and the most perfect oranges for the altar. Eliza ironed the white tablecloth and the white lace to cover the altar. Mr. Rodrigues brought out and cleaned the square wooden boxes for the altar. They hired other people to come and help with cleaning the house, painting, washing and dusting. Mrs. Rodrigues was serious about having

Jesus as a guest, and the house had to be in perfect order to receive Him, along with the many townspeople who would stop by with their holiday wishes.

While the house was being cleaned, the cakes and cookies baked, and the *licor* made, Isabel was busy implementing her plan of how to get Santa's attention. Every day she would go to the back room of the second floor of their house where there was an opening to the terrace roof. There was a wooden ladder that her parents used to climb up to the terrace to dry clothes, or, during the harvest season, to dry crops. Isabel and her little sisters were not allowed to go up that ladder. It was the legend in the family that it was on that same ladder that Santa climbed down on Christmas Eve after he landed on the terrace from the sky.

No one in the island had actually ever seen Santa or how he traveled; as far as anyone knew, he descended from heaven on a rope. No child ever dared to question this at least not out loud. How he looked, how he actually came down from heaven was a gift for every child to imagine. Each of the Rodrigues children grew up with her own vision of what Santa looked like, and especially how he managed to remain unseen all these years. Sometimes they discussed their ideas of Santa and argued about it, but in the end their visions of Santa were their own and unique, cherished in their hearts. He was mysterious, he was kind, he was swift and loved all children. That was all they knew, and that was enough, until one day…

It was one of those magical afternoons when heaven itself seemed to have fallen to earth and blessed them with its largess and in the process inadvertently added to this Santa mystery. For months rumors had been flying around the island that one of the pack ships was planning to make a trip to the island directly from New Bedford. In the olden days, Raymond and Margaret remembered, these ships would come often with passengers, food, clothes, and all kinds of household items and even building materials, but now these trips were rare. Whenever a ship came, the Rodrigues family received packages from Margaret's family, and especially from her older sister, Mana.

"In those days," Mrs. Rodrigues would tell her children, "we felt more connected to America than to Portugal. It was America who practically fed us, clothed us, and showed us that we could have a better life. For Portugal, our island was just a tiny speck of land in the Atlantic ocean with no real worth. Most of us here have family in America, but few of us have family in Portugal. I was practically born there in America," she would say proudly.

At that the children would all get excited and would ask, "How is that, Mother? Tell us!" So their mother would tell them how in the Whaling Days, her ancestors had settled in New Bedford, having gone there as crew members on the whaling and other merchant ships. Her parents lived in New Bedford in America for many years, and her sister, Mana, was born in New Bedford. She, herself, was born just a couple of months after they arrived in Brava.

"So my beginnings were in America," she would say. Then she would add with a wisp of regret, "If only my father had waited just a few months before he decided to bring his family here, I would have been an American citizen just like Mana."

Everyone listening would fall silent pondering the "What if…." Sadness would come over them for what seemed a fateful twist in their history, but then Mrs. Rodrigues would say, "But, if I had been born in New Bedford, perhaps, I would have never met your father, and if I had never met your father, all of you would not have been born, so God knew what He was doing. What would the world do without you?"

It was indeed a very difficult leap for Isabel and her siblings to think of themselves as not existing. But Ida would promptly remind them, "Well, this is not really true. If Father had managed to arrive in New Bedford in his stowaway ship, then you could have met Father, and we would still be here."

Isabel would answer, "Yes, we would still be here, as we are, but richer and living in America." Then they would all burst out into raucous laughter.

Mr. Rodrigues' daring and desperate attempt to get to America by stowing away in a ship was legendary. He was only eighteen years old at the time, and he had had a terrible spat with his father, who himself had lived and worked in California. Young Raymond grew up knowing about life in America, and when a ship was going to New Bedford he had asked permission to go and try his luck. His parents had refused, but this did not stop Raymond. He made arrangements on his own and hid in the ship as it was sailing off. The ship, as it turned out, was filled with stowaways, many known to the captain, and many others unknown, like Raymond, who were trying to get a free passage.

According to Mr. Rodrigues, he never knew the whole story, but as he recalled after several days at sea, there was a big fight, about what he did not know; it seemed like an aborted mutiny. The captain became afraid that, with so many illegal passengers on his ship, some malcontent might turn him in to immigration, and he might be arrested as soon as they docked. The captain felt that he couldn't take the chance, so the ship turned around within a month of leaving the port of Furna.

"You see? It all worked out," Mrs. Rodrigues would conclude cheerfully.

Well, that magical afternoon the pack ship finally arrived. Mr. Rodrigues had gone to Furna, where the ship had docked the night before, to claim their packages and to get them through customs. This process always took the whole day.

It was about four o'clock in the afternoon when the island's only cargo truck arrived in the town. The truck stopped in front of their house, and a beaming Mr. Rodrigues got out calling for help to get the boxes out of the truck and up the stairs. By then, Mrs. Rodrigues and all her children and all the household help were practically spilling out of the windows and doors with anticipation, watching Mr. Rodrigues and two men struggling to get the boxes up the stairs. There were two huge boxes with widths wider than the doorway to the parlor. After struggling and turning each box this way and the other, they gave up at last and left the boxes at the top of the stairs in the entryway between the parlor and one of the bedrooms.

Then the frenzy began. "Get me a knife! Not that one, the kitchen knife!" Mr. Rodrigues yelled out in an attempt to get someone to bring him the right instrument to cut the strong rope that had kept the boxes intact throughout their long voyage. They kept bringing him every sharp object that they could find, while Mrs. Rodrigues began to dig into the sides of the cardboard box with her sharp sewing scissors. The children also helped expedite the process by peeling off thin layers of the tape with which their aunt had reinforced the boxes.

At last the boxes were ripped open, and as usual with these things, it became a free—for—all. Whatever you could grab first from the box, you claimed (at least temporarily) and put it in your pile. "Oh, look at this, Mother. Oh, how beautiful! Look! Look!" one of the girls would say, and then often there would be a struggle when two or more of the girls would get hold of the same item at the same time. This day, Ida came to an odd item at the bottom of one of the boxes.

"What is this?" she muttered to herself. It was nothing spectacular, and it would have gotten thrown out with the remains of the box if it weren't for Ida's curious nature. She picked it up and put it in her pile for later inspection.

After the frenzy had subsided, Mrs. Rodrigues inspected each child's pile to evaluate the appropriateness of the items, what needed to be shared with others and so forth. She came to the item and said to Ida, "What do you have here, Ida?"

She responded, "I don't really know. It was at the bottom of that box all by itself," she responded. It looked like a silhouette of a man in white cardboard that seemed to be folded onto itself and kept shut by a paper clip.

Mrs. Rodrigues released the paperclip and unfolded the paper back onto itself, and all the children, including Mrs. Rodrigues, exclaimed, "Oh! Oh!" It was a three–dimensional portrait of a jolly Santa Claus in his red suit and black boots, with long white hair and spectacles, having a ballooned, honeycombed paper belly and lugging a huge, heavy bag overflowing with toys. That was their very first acquaintance with Santa, and he was indeed a much, much fatter *Nhõ Bedjo*, Mister Old Man than they had ever imagined.

This created a problem in the minds of the young little Rodrigueses who wondered how such an old fat man like that was able to come down those rickety old ladders from the terrace. In no time, however, their active imaginations began to work on the question and each found in her mind an acceptable explanation. Isabel became secretly elated with this new vision of Santa, *This is a very rich Nhõ Bedjo. He will surely bring my shoes!* she thought. This cardboard–and–paper Santa immediately found a place of honor on the altar along with the Christmas card.

Isabel, by now, had established her routine, and every morning and evening, with the picture of her shoes in hand, she would stand at the foot of the ladder and yell out at the top of her lungs, "Oh, dear Old Man, this is what I want you to bring me this year. These shoes!" She would lift her arms holding the picture and look straight up toward the patch of clear sky showing in from the opening to the terrace above. "Please, Santa, I would be very much obliged if you could bring me these shoes with a red round balloon and an orange lollipop." She did this faithfully every day as though it were a prayer. Often at the end of her request, she would list her wishes to make sure that there was no confusion. "Three things: these shoes, a red round balloon, and an orange lollipop."

Of course, siblings being who they are, the story of Isabel's Christmas wish spread throughout the neighborhood and quickly it became fodder for some teasing when she played in the park.

Prayers from the Heart

…Dear Children! I invite you again to pray with the heart,

Mary's message to Međugorje in Pray with the Heart!

by Fr. Slavko Barbarić

At last Christmas Eve came. In the afternoon on Christmas Eve, the altar was finally set up in the living room. The corn seedlings were now small plants, thick and green, the oranges were round and plump, and the statue of the child Jesus was gleaming. Mr. Rodrigues came home with some candles, and Mrs. Rodrigues arranged them throughout the altar. There were some red and yellow roses that Mrs. Rodrigues pinned all around on the white lace that covered the altar. She brought out her grandmother's nativity set. There were several figurines of shepherds running and kneeling. There were five figurines of little sheep looking lost. One had a broken leg that she had fixed with a string. There was a figurine of baby Jesus' mother, bent over, wearing a white dress and a long blue cape. There was another of a man named Joseph, whom Mr. Rodrigues told the children was Jesus' adopted father. There were a mule and a cow lying down chewing hay. There was one of Baby Jesus with no clothes on, lying on a bed of golden straw. Oh, yes, there was one of an angel that Mrs. Rodrigues put at the top of the altar just below the big star that she had made from a gold candy wrapper. She placed all these figurines around that of the Baby Jesus and His mother and father. At the base of the altar, a little way from the shepherds, she put the figurines of the three kings that came from far away to visit and bring Jesus presents.

"This is how it was that night in Bethlehem, the town where Jesus was born," she said reverently. Then she lit the candles and said a prayer out loud to welcome Jesus, and she asked Him to bless their home. She also said a prayer for her two older sons, Andy and Joseph, who were away studying, and for her eldest daughter, Leyla, now married and living in Portuguese Guinea, in mainland Africa. Mr. Rodrigues and Mrs. Rodrigues then silently said another prayer and tears rolled down their cheeks. The children became solemn and bowed their heads also in prayer. They were now praying for little Meg, who had died long ago before any of the children were born, nevertheless, she was never forgotten. This was all that Margaret let her husband and her children know about what went on in her head and in her heart.

For Margaret Rodrigues Christmas and the Feast of the Holy Spirit, Pentecost, were the most beautiful feast days. She would say, "The most beautiful," because there were no other words to describe the essence of these feasts. These were the beliefs that kept her with one foot on earth and the other in heaven. In both of these feasts the Blessed Mother was a silent but central figure. Margaret's most cherished possessions were her grandmother's nativity set and her mother's statue of the Child Jesus. Not just because these articles were used by them, but because these were articles of faith which, when she meditated upon their meaning, spoke to her and gave her own life a sense of purpose. She would look at the figurines representing The Holy Family: Infant Jesus, mother Mary and father Joseph; and she, who had borne nine children, couldn't help but identify herself with Mary, and her heart ached for her.

When meditating on the nativity she would think, *All of my children were born in my bed, in the same bed where they had been conceived, and here is Mary, the mother of Jesus, the mother of our God—made man, giving birth in a stable, putting her baby in a feeding trough, with no female relatives to attend to her and comfort her. With no one near to make her even a cup of coffee. And Mary, never complained, never fretted about the situation, never worried. She put herself completely in the hands of God. Giving birth in a stable on a cold night in Bethlehem did not shake her faith in God or perhaps cause her to ask why. She was one with God. This is why she was truly "full of grace."* She would ponder how she too could be like Mary and trust completely in God.

Margaret knew that while birthing was painful, it was also joyous and hopeful: Hope for the best for the baby being born, whose life and whose destiny God alone knew. And surely Mary was full of hope for her Baby Jesus whose destiny was known only to His Almighty Father.

"Joy to the world, the Savior's come. Let earth receive her King...and heaven and nature sing..." The Holy Papa, her Spouse, the Holy Spirit, sent choirs of angels and lit up the universe to announce the birth of the Wonderful, Excelsior, King of Peace, Immanuel! Margaret wondered, *Did Mary hear the fanfare going on outside in the hills? Did she hear the chorus of angels? Or, like any other mother, was Mary concerned with keeping her baby warm?* Margaret, in her heart, thought that perhaps Mary was not aware of all the fanfare going on in the hills; that what the shepherds heard she did not hear, perhaps she was only listening to the beating of His heart, the rhythm of His breathing, the movement of His bowels, the passing of His water.

Margaret would ponder the first time that the Baby Jesus sucked from Mary's tender breasts, and how glad she must have been to be able to feed Him. Did she sing Him a lullaby when He cried? Did she burp Him when He was colicky? She perhaps even counted His toes and His fingers and checked His body all over to make sure that He was perfect, and He was the most perfect human baby that had ever been born. These things Margaret had also done after the birth of each one of her children and as she did, she had thought of Mary. Margaret's children were also all well, except for one who had a slight defect in one foot—but for that she had faith that God would answer her prayer in due time.

Like Mary, Margaret did not hear the sounds of the *foguetes,* the fireworks, that her husband would fire up from the steps of the park announcing the birth of each one of their children. Nor was she aware of the numerous rounds of their best *grogo* that he would offer to his friends who came by to congratulate them. She, like Mary, was quietly attending to her newborn.

Throughout the year, Mary remained close to Margaret's heart. Margaret would often pray in Latin, the language of her Church, *Ave Maria, gratia plena, Dominus tecum, benedicta tu i mulieribus, Et benedictus fructus ventris tui, Jesus, Sancta Maria, Mater Dei, Ora pro nobis peccatoribus. Nunc et in hora mortis nostrae*[4]. *Amen,* asking Mary to intercede with her Son for Margaret and her loved ones.

Because Margaret had been orphaned when she was just a child, Mary had become her spiritual mother, who nurtured her and prayed with her, interceding incessantly on her behalf. Margaret felt that Mary understood her: Mary understood her needs, her worries, her pains, and her longings. Mary, as a woman, a wife, and a mother, had gone through it all. When Margaret sewed a pair of pants for her boys, or sewed a button on her husband's shirt, or put up a hem on the girls' dresses, she thought of Mary doing the same for the Child Jesus and her husband, Joseph. When Margaret packed the suitcases for her two boys to go off to school, she thought of Mary and she put them in Mary's hands, under her protection because she knew that her spiritual mother was their spiritual mother who would watch over them, who would keep them safe, and who would direct their lives, their spirits, to her Son. Mary always came through for her and would for her family too.

Margaret looked to Mary on another level as well. Mary was but a shadow in the Gospel. Margaret felt that she too was but a shadow in her community—she hardly ever ventured out from her house and sometimes wondered what her life was worth. Mary may seem to have been powerless, but her power rested in her total love for her Son, her total devotion to God. The world was changed by her love and acceptance of what God asked of her. Margaret too wanted her life to make a difference and heard in her heart Mary saying, as she had said at the wedding in Cana, "Look to my Son. Do whatever He tells you." She wanted to emulate the quiet wisdom of Mary. So she prayed, *Oh Holy Spirit, give me the gift of wisdom, so that I will always know and choose right over wrong, so that I will always choose Christ over anything else.*

Mary was *gratia plena* as the angel greeted her, which Margaret understood as Mary's having all the seven gifts of the Holy Spirit and perhaps all the treasures of her Son's kingdom. She set up the altar with reverence thinking of all these things.[5]

After Christmas Day, in the next several weeks, a priest would come first to bless the altar and then lead the people gathered around to pray the rosary. Mr. Rodrigues hardly ever participated in these prayers. And as far as anyone could tell, even though he attended the Sunday Mass faithfully, he did not believe in bringing church into the home; at least, that was what he liked people to think. So, he met the men out in the park, engaged in political debates, speculated on the weather, the rains, and business in general.

For the rest of the year, Mr. Rodrigues had his best friend, Isabel's godfather, over every evening after dinner to listen to the radio. They would listen to a news program originating from London. The program always began with the tolling of the bells from one of the abbeys in London. "The voice of London is the voice of the free world," Mr. Rodrigues would say. It connected them to the outside world; it connected them with those who were really important, who were running, or "ruining" the world, as Mrs. Rodrigues would say when the news was about war breaking out in this or that part of the world.

Most of the news did not concern them and their little world; little of the news disrupted the rhythm of their lives, except in the case of World War II when no pack ships dared to cross the Atlantic and they were forgotten and abandoned. Now the faint rumblings for the independence of the Portuguese colonies were beginning again to shake up their world. But, in any case, during Christmas season, the radio was moved out of the living room to elsewhere in the house. The evening praying of the rosary was now the more important thing.

Margaret, her neighbors, a few of her relatives who lived in town, and sometimes visitors that came all the way from the Parish of *Nossa Senhora do Monte* (Our Lady of the Mount), a good two hours away, would gather at their Christmas altar for the rosary.

The people from *Nossa Senhora do Monte* were Margaret's distant relatives and often stayed overnight. These were the relatives who were closely tied to America. Most of them had lived for many years in California and also New Bedford, and the older ones had spent most of their youths in America and then come home to *Nossa Senhora do Monte* to retire. They lived in big houses and their customs and their language were different. They ate 'squash pies'! They were always saying, "Yah, yah." Their conversation was peppered with English words like *zipper* and *machine* this and *machine* that. People laughed when they heard these people from *Campo*—the woods—visiting the town. They had a habit of chewing gum, and their pockets jingled with money and bulged with sweets that they called *kandé*. They wore extravagant looking clothes; they were oversized, often blonde and blue eyed. Mr. Rodrigues attributed his wife's extraordinary good looks to this lineage. But these relatives were considered by the town's people as "backwards," and sometimes an embarrassment. Margaret, however, was proud of her *Nossa Senhora do Monte* relatives and enjoyed their company.

During the overnight visits of these relatives during the Christmas holidays, the Rodrigues girls had to triple up in a bed to make room for them. Most of the children delighted in all the buzz and excitement and the attention that they got from the relatives in their household. Isabel, however, tried to stay away as much as possible. She came to dread these intrusions into their family life. These relatives, it seemed to Isabel, tended to take over the house. The windows overlooking the park and the avenue were always full of them, and any Rodrigues, big or small, had a hard time inching her way to find a spot with a view. But what upset Isabel the most was that these relatives were enamored of her cherubic cheeks and couldn't get enough of the thrill of pinching them.

"Oh, look at those cheeks of Isabel! See how red they are. They are like cherries." This infuriated Isabel. The more they pinched her cheeks the redder they became, and that won her the nickname of *cerejinha*, the little cherry face. Her mother, on the other hand, loved the nickname—the cherubic cherry face spoke to her of Isabel's general good health. She even tried to call Isabel *cerejinha*, but Isabel quickly put a stop to it.

That did not stop one of their neighbors from slapping her with a new nickname also related to her prominent cheeks. One could hear the neighbor calling Isabel at a distance when she wanted Isabel to do an errand for her, "Lua cheia! Oh! Lua cheia, come here." Well, her cheeks were a curse, Isabel was convinced of it, and if it wasn't "little cherry face" it was now "full moon."

Her mother tried to comfort her by saying; "You know, Isabel, what you may consider sometimes a curse, may in fact be a blessing." Mrs. Rodrigues never actually explained this blessing in disguise, and Isabel dared not ask.

In general, Isabel stayed away from her *Nossa Senhora do Monte* relatives. She did feel attracted to the beauty of their altar and in her own little way had developed a devotion to the Child Jesus who was depicted in the statue under the glass dome. Although she felt sorry for Him for wearing a dress, Isabel thought that He looked beautiful and in a way that dress set him apart from any boy that she had ever seen. It made Him look '*out of this world*,' which, in fact, He was.

She prayed the rosary—that is, she mumbled a few Hail Marys here and there and also the Our Father—but where she distinguished herself was in the singing. She had a strong, clear soprano voice that dominated in singing "Salve Regina" and "Silent Night." When singing "Salve Regina," Isabel often imagined herself actually in front of the Blessed Mother, saying to her, simply, "Hello, Queen, how are you?" This was also the case with "Silent Night." Her mind would wander and she would find herself in front of that manger in Bethlehem, looking at the star just as the shepherds did. Often she would be so captured by her imagination that she would continue to sing long after everyone else had stopped, which caused her considerable embarrassment when she realized it.

On Christmas Eve, with dresses, shirts, and pants pressed, and shoes polished, Mrs. Rodrigues served supper extra early. She and Mr. Rodrigues sneaked out to finalize their Christmas shopping. Eliza put Isabel, Ida and Mandy, to bed for a nap and then lay down herself. Isabel and her sisters, including Eliza and Fern, were so excited with the anticipation of Santa's descent from the terrace that they could hardly sleep.

While everyone was napping, however, Isabel snuck in a last trip to the ladder by the terrace opening. She looked up, and she could see a clear patch of the evening sky studded with stars. She made her request to Santa one last time. Then she stopped by the altar, which was situated right on the opposite side of the wall that divided her room from the parlor. She knelt down, bowed her head, and whispered her request again. Then, suddenly, at the nape of her neck, she felt a tingling sensation that rippled gently down her spine; she jerked back to see if there was anyone there. There was no one that she could see. Her heart racing, she scurried back to her room and cuddled against Ida, who was asleep. She buried her face in her pillow, but kept peeking now and again in an attempt to catch a glimpse of the presence that had touched her body. She kept this going for a long while until her weary body succumbed, and she, too, fell asleep.

The Reluctant Angel

...Let all the angels of God worship him.

Hebrews 1:6

It had all begun with her First Communion, two years ago. Isabel remembered that day with mixed feelings. She and several other children had been preparing for over a year for this event. As babies, they all had been baptized as members of Jesus Christ's Church, and they were presented to the Church by the faith of their parents. Now they had to begin their own journey, making their own choices. They were seven years old, and the Church looked upon them as little people with the power of reason. The way it was explained to them was that they now understood what was right and what was wrong and could consciously make a good or a bad choice. So, before receiving Holy Communion, which in the Catholic Church is receiving the actual body, blood, soul, and divinity of Jesus Christ, they had first to prepare their hearts and go through the sacrament of Confession to be forgiven for any sins, becoming completely pure and white in their souls to receive God. This internal purity was expressed outwardly by wearing white.

Isabel's mother had gone to great lengths to redesign Fern's Communion dress, which was Eliza's before that, and Leyla's before Eliza's. She wanted to make the dress look brand new, and, to fit Isabel's sense of style, she concocted an elaborate long veil made of tulle recycled from an old petticoat. Isabel would be so beautiful! But, as these things often go, a few days before the event, Isabel developed an abscess in one of her molars, and on the day of her First Communion, one side of her chin had ballooned up. Throughout the ceremony Isabel held her head slightly tilted to hide her infected cheek, and her pained expression gave her the pining look that was common among angel portraits. This angelic demeanor did not go unnoticed. Soon, much to her dismay, she was in demand.

Whenever a holiday, such as Christmas, was approaching and she saw someone from church come to the house requesting to speak specifically to her mother in private, Isabel would cringe. This was also the case when there was a wedding and the bride came by with the same request. Invariably, they all wanted her to serve as a little angel, or to be a part of the bridal party carrying the satin embroidered white cushion for the bride to kneel upon in church.

Her father also loved to volunteer her whenever there was a solemn occasion and the governor or some other official, from the capital or from Portugal, made a visit. On these occasions, Isabel would be asked to recite a poem, present the official with a bouquet of flowers, sing a *morna*, a traditional slow and melancholic ballad, or even reproduce a part that she had learned in the summer variety shows.

Isabel was never asked if she wanted to do these things. Her mother would get heavily involved in teaching her the poems and songs and rehearsing with her and also sewing the various dresses and costumes that would be required. Isabel loved to participate in the summer variety shows that the young people put on with the help of the church, but being an angel or the cushion bearer was most painful for her. Yet, she knew that it gave her parents great pleasure, and since these things were expected of her, she always learned her part and did the best she could without a big fuss.

Being part of the bridal party was awkward but no big deal for her. Most of the time she felt embarrassed walking in the street in front of the bride on her way from the bride's house to church, and then back again accompanied by invited guests and all the uninvited curious townspeople. It was a huge public spectacle that in her culture was common. Isabel's cheeks would turn redder than any tomato that anyone had ever seen, and she would lower her eyes so as not to see all the people on the sidelines who were trying to get her attention. She would keep a steady pace that she had been drilled on for a few days before. Indeed, she appeared as the perfect little angel.

Being an angel in church was another matter. It caused her some internal turmoil. "What do angels do?" she had asked. They had discussed the subject of angels in her Sunday School class.

"Angels are spirits, also created by God, who work for God," one of her Sunday School teachers had explained. "Angels do different things that God wants done." In Isabel's house was a picture depicting a beautiful angel guiding two little children across a dangerous bridge. They were the guardian angels. She was also familiar with the angel Gabriel who spoke to Mary and told her that she was going to have Jesus. And, in her family they were also acquainted with 'the angel of the boot,' as Ida called it.

Ida was born with a defect in her left foot—it was flipped over so that when she started to walk the top of her foot touched the ground and the sole of the foot remained exposed to air. This defect, however, did not stop Ida. Although she walked with a limp, she could run as quickly as the best and became her neighborhood's champion at spinning the top. This handicap never prevented her from doing anything, and in all appearances she was not affected by it. One day, when the same woman who had bellowed out from her veranda, "*Lua cheia*" to Isabel, called out to Ida, "*Pé torto, Oh, Pé torto!*" (Crooked foot, Oh, crooked foot!), Ida, without missing a beat, stood up as straight as her two feet would allow and replied, "Don't call me crooked foot. No! Leyla named me Ida. Call me Ida." The woman was partially amused and stunned by Ida's response, and that put an end to that.

Not too long after that incident, on a late Saturday afternoon just as the sun was setting, what appeared to be a tall, black man approached Mrs. Rodrigues while she was working on her front flower garden. Eliza and Fern were helping her while Isabel, Ida, and Mandy were playing on the sidewalk in front of the garden. He asked Mrs. Rodrigues, "Is that little girl with the limp your daughter?"

Mrs. Rodrigues stopped her gardening and looked up at the stranger. The sun was low on the horizon and was directly behind the man so that she was partially blinded by the red glow of the sun. Mrs. Rodrigues replied, "Yes."

The man then told her, "Get her a strong leather boot that goes up over her ankles. Keep it laced up tight and let her wear the boot day and night. In a few months to a year, her foot will turn over and she will be able to walk and run normally, just like your other daughters."

The man immediately took his leave, and Mrs. Rodrigues yelled out after him, "Thank you. What is your name? Where do you live?" The man did not respond, nor did he turn around, but kept walking up the steps to the park and disappeared. Whenever Mrs. Rodrigues retold the story, she became teary–eyed and would grab Ida, holding her daughter on her lap, caressing and kissing the top of her head. "It was an angel, Raymond, I tell you!"

Mr. Rodrigues only half–believed the angel part of the story. Nevertheless, the next day he took Ida to the cobblers who made a pair of boots exactly as the man had described. Ida's foot slowly was set back to the normal position, and now two years later, Ida was always eager to challenge her friends and even Isabel to a race up and down the avenue. Sometimes, when Ida prayed she rubbed her foot. Isabel suspected that she was thanking her "angel of the boot."

So Isabel could understand that angels work for God, but her teacher had also said that, "there is a group of angels who surround God in His throne and just adore Him."

"What is adore?" Isabel had asked. She couldn't under-stand what these angels actually did.

The Sunday School teacher shook her head slightly and then said, "To adore is to know that God created us. To adore is to love God. Yes," she affirmed, and continued, "to love God. To love God totally, always and without ceasing and in silence." She said this knowing that the children would not understand because she herself did not understand it. She was just repeating what she had been taught, and trying to keep the children quiet.

Now, once again Isabel was to be an angel. She was anxious and excited about Santa, but not about being an angel at Christmas Eve Mass. At rehearsals, all the little angels were told that all they had to do was to kneel by the crèche, keep their hands folded as in prayer and sing the Glo–O–O–Oria at the appropriate times. Otherwise, they were to keep up an angelic gaze at the doll that represented the Baby Jesus lying in the manger and try not to cough amidst the heavy clouds of incense that the priest would surely be sending their way.

Isabel understood that she was playing one of those adoring angels because she was a part of the group of angels who surround the crèche with Baby Jesus. She knew she was playing the part of God's inner circle of angels whose job was to adore Him, but how would she do that?

"You do that by imitating the angels. Bow deeply as a sign of adoration of the Lord. Keep quiet thinking about Baby Jesus. Angels of God worship God all the time, they are very loyal to God, and they are very obedient. Try to think about this when you are up there near the crèche," their angel coach told them.

This question of adoration became so problematic for the little angels that the Sunday School teacher asked the priest to come in one day. The priest had a very simple way of explaining the concept. He said, "Say the prayer that Jesus taught us. When we pray 'the Our Father' we adore God. Because of Jesus, God has adopted us as His children. So we are thankful to Him. We recognize that He is All Good. Think of the words carefully as you say them. This is adoration."

Most of this went over their little heads, but they understood some of it and kept their hands folded in prayer. "Gaze constantly at the crèche and look like you are enjoying it. As if you are in love," their angel coach finally said.

"And how was that?" they would ask. It was pure embarrassment. It was more embarrassing than parading down the street in the wedding party with all the people looking at you. But embarrassing or not they all tried to do what they were told, some more successfully than others in their own rendition of the 'in love' look. Isabel hated it.

It was about eleven fifteen at night on Christmas Eve when Mrs. Rodrigues got everybody up to prepare for the midnight Mass. Eliza and Fern dressed Isabel up in the white crepe dress and tightly strapped the papier-mâché wings on her back. After much protest from Isabel, Eliza brushed down her tangles of shiny, black hair and placed the special hair band with little wax flowers near her forehead.

In church, Isabel tried to do as she had rehearsed, and on cue all the other little angels began to sing the Gloria, except Isabel. She kept her lips puckered in the "O" position with no sound coming out of them. Other times she would have dominated the voices of her fellow little angels, today she was feeling tired, agitated, and plain not in the mood. In fact, throughout the Mass she was feeling 'anxious.' All that she was thinking about was, *When is this thing going to end,* so that she could race home and see what Santa had brought.

She looked down at her feet and almost felt the soft leather of her new Lisbon shoes caressing her feet. She was excited and it showed. Her sisters, who were sitting not too far from the altar, were worried and tried to signal her to behave. She was pulling on her curls, whispering in the ears of her fellow angels, and once even wiped her forehead with the hem of her skirt, which she had pulled up so high that her underpants were showing. One of the angel coaches managed to quietly get near Isabel and pinch her to behave, but that only caused Isabel to respond with a loud "Ouch!" She met her disapproving sisters' eyes and hastily went back to her angelic pose out of sheer embarrassment.

The Epiphany

Then, suddenly, the voice of God, like divine music,
rose and swelled throughout paradise.

The Littlest Angel by Charles Tazewell

In silent adoration, with her head bowed down, Isabel
began to pray The Lord's Prayer, "Our Father, who art in
heaven, hallowed be Thy Name…" She kept praying this
over and over in her head and consequently she became very
sleepy and would have toppled over, if not for something
she heard that caught her imagination.

A group of children was reenacting the story of the
birth of Jesus. Isabel remembered what her mother had told
her about Christmas being a time that we get many gifts,
but also give many—a time to receive and to give. She realized that all she had been doing was asking to receive. She
had not given any thought about giving anything to anyone.
She recalled that all the shepherds on her altar at home, and
also in the story that she was now listening to, had some
gift for Baby Jesus. One shepherd had a baby lamb, another
had a jar of honey, and another had some eggs nestled in
his shepherd's hat. The kings themselves all had something.

She did not understand what the kings' gifts were for, but she figured that they must be good and important gifts if the kings, themselves, were carrying them.

I wish that I had a gift to give. But what? she thought, rather sad, confused, and tearful. Isabel bent down to grab the hem of her skirt to wipe her tears. As she did so, she noticed a row of bare, black, little feet in front of her. She blinked, and realized for the first time that evening that crowded on the steps going up to the altar where she was standing with the other little angels, and also at the side door going out to the sacristy, were several children dressed in clean, but patched up clothes. Isabel recognized most of them.

There was Tonia, a little girl who was in her class and whom she often played with at recess. There were also Zé, Jony, Lulucha and Carmen; they were all from her school. These were kids with whom she was friendly during the school year, and played with during recess, but outside school they lived in very different worlds. She knew very little about these schoolmates, not even where they lived or who their parents were. Once out of school she hardly ever gave a thought about them. They belonged to a different group, usually poorer and *mestizo,* and it was all right to play with them at school but one would not socialize with them at any other time. These were the kids whose parents Isabel's parents would hire to work in their fields. They would never come to her house to play, and if they did come, they used the side door, never the front door.

It was odd that she was thinking about this now. Her eyes met Tonia's, and they exchanged glances of recognition and friendship. But Tonia was barefoot, and she wore a rather ugly man's jacket over her shoulder. She wore that coat all the time to school, and now she was wearing it in church on Christmas Eve. *Could this be the best outfit that she has?* Isabel thought in disbelief. She also glanced at Jony, Carmen and Lulucha. They smiled at her and she smiled back at them. Jony blushed! That made Isabel blush too. There was something about Jony; he always blushed and fiddled with something in his pockets whenever there was the slightest exchange between them. Isabel also felt less than her usual confident self around Jony. But even though they lived in a very small community, they might as well have lived over 1,000 miles apart. There was an invisible abyss that divided their worlds and each seemed to know it instinctively.

But what was more puzzling to Isabel was that they were barefoot and wearing clothes with patches—their normal school clothes.

Isabel frowned and thought, *They must be really poor if they are here on Christmas Eve barefoot like that.* She was amazed at this discovery. Of course she had seen many children in church barefoot before, but she had never thought much about it. Suddenly she was filled with a sense of urgency—and perhaps of deep contrition.

Isabel's Gift

Bless the shoes that take me to and from
Up and down and everywhere

Prayer for a Child by Rachel Field

Isabel was puzzled and confused by this new revelation. Her little heart ached, not like it did when she thought about Dee and her Lisbon–made shoes when her heart felt small and tight, but it ached to the point that it felt that it—it was going to burst.

She felt sad about Tonia. She and Tonia were in the same grade, and they had been in the same class since they began *cartilha,* kindergarten. Tonia did not live in town; Isabel had heard that she lived in *Djan de Nole,* which was up in the mountains, past the stone quarry. From the windows of her house, Isabel could see the stone quarry to the left, and to the right of it, higher up, were some beautiful white houses in *Djan de Nole,* but she was sure that they were not where Tonia lived. Isabel searched her mind to remember some details about Tonia. Well, she walked with a limp so that she was not very good in hopscotch. She liked to learn but she did not always come to school with homework all done; as Isabel now remembered she had a lot of heavy chores to do—not like Isabel's chores—before she could go to school.

She was quiet, but pleasant to be with. She also participated in the *merenda escolar*, the school lunch. The lunch was free, and it was only for the very poor children and those who lived far away. Isabel was not eligible, but that didn't stop her from wanting to participate whenever there was a chance. This past year she had eaten twice in the school lunch. It happened that whenever someone was absent, the teacher would ask if there was anyone who was hungry and wanted the lunch. Isabel always raised her hand—not because she was hungry, but because she loved the merenda's *chachupa* (dehulled corn cooked with kale, salted pork, beans, and spices—a favorite dish that was served often for dinner), which she thought was the tastiest that she had ever eaten. On these occasions she would sit next to Tonia and they would be like best buddies.

Tonia was also in the group of girls who made up Isabel's inner circle of friends at recess time. They would share their snack: Isabel's white bread for Tonia's *gufongo*, cornbread wrapped in banana leaves and baked in hot ashes, Isabel's piece of sugar cane for Tonia's often-over-ripe cucumber.

She enjoyed Tonia's company, but once the school day was over they said their goodbyes until the next day or until the next year. Tonia would take a sharp left and begin to climb the mountain toward *Djan de Nole*, and Isabel would take the short walk straight ahead ending up at the park and at her house, forgetting about Tonia—as though Tonia had never existed until Isabel saw her again.

Poor Tonia. I wonder if she asked Nhō Bedjo for anything? I wonder if… Isabel's train of thought was interrupted by the incense that suddenly covered her face. She coughed a little and blessed herself. The priest, having sanctified the altar and the gifts on the altar with the incense, began to disperse clouds of incense first at the crèche and the little angels and then to the general group of believers.

Perhaps Nhō Bedjo doesn't go to every house. Nhō Bedjo maybe does not go to Tonia's house. Could it be that she does not know enough to ask? After all, Mother said that you need to ask. She felt consoled by that though—well, half-consoled.

She looked at the crèche; she looked at the shepherds all bringing gifts, and then she thought about how she had been asking Santa about new shoes. She thought about her mother's story about the magic of this night and how *to give is the same thing as to receive.* She had not understood it then, but now her heart opened up and she sadly thought, *It is too late now for Tonia. It is too late now to give her anything.* Right then and there, she made a resolution that her friendship with Tonia was going to change. She and Tonia were going to be just as good friends as she and Dee were.

Then, suddenly, her precious Lisbon–made shoes did not seem that important anymore, and she asked herself, *Do I really need the latest style imported shoes from Lisbon that I have been pestering Santa about all these weeks? How many sandals, like the ones I am wearing that Nhō Mané Sapatero made right here in Brava, would my Lisbon shoes buy?* Immediately, she saw ten happy little girls all with Tonia's face dancing with their sandals. Isabel smiled and asked herself, *How many plastic sandals from Senegal that vendors peddle around in the streets could my Lisbon—made shoes buy?* And immediately she saw a multitude of little boys and girls walking happily on a dusty road with their brand new plastic sandals.

Isabel smiled and she took a deep breath. Then she looked at the Baby Jesus in the crèche, and she knew what she needed to do—what He was asking her to do—to become a "real" angel for Him. She looked up to heaven and amidst all the incense and the Glorias, she gave up in her heart her Lisbon—made shoes in exchange for all those plastic sandals. The ache in her heart that she had first experienced when she began to envy her best friend's shoes vanished, and her heart expanded. She felt her papier—mâché wings come to life; they fluttered lightly sending a cool breeze up and around her face. She felt her feet ascend, and she was standing on a thin layer of air. She looked at her old sandals, and they seemed to sparkle. Isabel folded her hands in prayer and joined the choir singing "*Gloria in excelsis*" with all her might. Her heart was so filled with love that it expanded even further. It first claimed her whole chest, and then her whole body. It kept expanding, joining with her fellow little angels, then with her school friends, and then with everyone in the church and beyond. Her oblation from the heart had joined her with the world as she sang in unison with heaven and nature of the glory of God.

Nhõ Bedjo is Come

You better watch out, you better not cry. You better watch out, I'm telling you why. Santa Claus is coming to town.

Popular Christmas song by J. Fred Coots and
Henry Gillespie

On the way home after Mass, Isabel was blissfully quiet, but no one seemed to notice. Eliza held her hand, and they all walked silently back home. As they were getting near their house, everyone picked up the pace in excitement. Fern teasingly broke the silence, "Well, Isabel, do you think that you are going to get your shoes?"

"What? What shoes?" Isabel answered in a daze. They all turned their heads toward her in amazement.

"What shoes?" cried out Eliza incredulously, bending down to look straight at Isabel's face.

"The ones that you have been asking Santa for!" reminded little Mandy.

"Oh, Oh! Those shoes! Of course!" she said simply.

The children ran the next block home. Their parents were right behind them. Their house was ghostly. Its white stucco frame glowed against the starlit sky. Inside the house all was dark. All was quiet. All was serene. And suddenly, as if by magic, the house was awakened from its slumber and was lit up from top to bottom, buzzing with children's laughter and cries.

They all galloped straight up the stairs to their bedrooms, and with a flick of the light switch each child scampered to her side of the bed and to her boot. There were "Oohs" and "Ahhs" and "Oh my!" Ida and Mandy's boots were full. They both had a doll, a balloon and a lollipop. Fern and Eliza got new, identical sweaters, with perfume for Eliza and chocolates for Fern.

Isabel stood still in shock. She held her boot with both her hands and turned it upside down. All that fell out were two fat drops of tears rolling down her face. Isabel's boot was totally empty. Her parents stood at the door watching her closely. The other kids had not noticed. Isabel stood there with her little wings now drooping down her shoulders and began to cry. Her tear—filled eyes met her parents.'

Mrs. Rodrigues went quietly to her and put her arms around her. "It must have been a mistake," she said and kissed her forehead.

Mr. Rodrigues reassured, "*Nhō Bedjo* must have made a mistake! Tomorrow I will get you something special. Don't worry!" he added consolingly.

Isabel's whimpering alerted her sisters to her predicament. They were all stunned.

"*Nhō Bedjo* was mixed up, I am sure," said Eliza, herself a bit confused, and sending a biting look toward her parents.

"Come, Isabel. Come and help me light up the candles on the altar," her mother said.

As Isabel was being ushered out of her bedroom, she looked back at Ida and Mandy, happy with their gifts. Her whimpering became a loud cry, and her mother and father quickly whisked her off to the parlor.

Mrs. Rodrigues carefully lit the candles on the altar, one by one. The altar slowly came to life. Isabel looked at the figures of the child Jesus, the shepherds and the angels with a new understanding, and her little heart burst with love. Tears of joy now coursed down her cheeks.

"Oh, oh, don't cry. Look, Isabel! Look, there is a box in front of the altar," Mr. Rodrigues exclaimed. "What could that be, Margaret?"

"I don't know," Mrs. Rodrigues answered. Isabel noticed that it was a box—a shoebox! She quickly picked up the box and read the scribbling in red crayon, "For Isabel."

Isabel, her big eyes gleaming in expectation, looked at her father, then at her mother, and then abruptly pulled off the cover of the box. Her mouth dropped open. Her eyes grew bigger, and her wings perked up. For a moment she hesitated and then she could only say, "Oh! Oh!" in a whisper. The other children all came in and huddled around her. The bottom of the shoebox was lined with gold paper and in it lay a pair of knee–high red socks with fluffy decorative tassels, much in style on the island.

"No shoes!" Mrs. Rodrigues said, looking almost apologetically at Isabel.

"No shoes, but socks!" Isabel replied enthusiastically and continued, "*Nhō Bedjo* did bring me shoes, but I gave them away." Isabel rattled on trying to explain to everyone what had happened to the shoes, without success.

"What do you mean—you gave them away?" her father asked mystified. Isabel looked at her mother, and her mother bent over. Isabel whispered in her mother's ear.

"What?" her mother reacted loudly. Isabel kept her gaze firmly on her mother's eyes while nodding her head. Mr. Rodrigues looked at his wife. She signaled to him to let the subject drop.

Then Isabel said, "I have shoes. Look, how pretty my sandals are. Let me try them with these pretty socks."

Isabel's parents and sisters shook their heads—Isabel was often hard to understand and her fantasies sometimes took strange twists.

Isabel grabbed one foot of the socks and felt that there was something smooth inside. She slipped her hand all the way to the toe. She grabbed something and brought it out.

"It is my balloon!" she said in awe.

"A red, round balloon just like mine!" Ida noted.

Then Isabel took the other sock and noticed that there was something hard inside. She again slipped her hand all the way in and grabbed something and brought it out.

"It is my lollipop!" she cried out while holding it up for everyone to see.

"An orange lollipop, just like the ones that Mandy and I got!" Ida again noted.

"Oh, I see something else way down there, Isabel," Fern pointed out, giving a wink to Eliza. Isabel brought her face practically inside the box and took off the paper that was lining the box, and there it was, a small square of fabric. She picked it up and unfolded it and looked around in surprise, "Oh! A kerchief! Oh my goodness, a kerchief!" Mr. and Mrs. Rodrigues looked puzzled, but Eliza and Fern were beaming.

"Look Isabel, if you fold it like so, you can wear it like a headband," said Fern.

"Or, you can use it like so, knotted in front, or knotted in the back under your hair," Eliza demonstrated.

"Or, you can just pin it around your waist and let it fly in the wind when you walk, just like Leyla used to do," reminded Fern.

Isabel immediately put it on her head tied under her hair.

"It looks very pretty!" Mandy said.

"It is prettier than Dee's!" Ida added.

Isabel sat on the floor facing the altar, her body tilted back, resting on her arms. Extending legs outward, and pulling up her long dress, she admired, with a gleam in her eyes, her feet. She felt her wings spread out like an eagle's soaring, her cheeks in flame. She looked at the glowing altar, she looked at her mother, she looked at her father, and she looked at her sisters and said, "I wish that Andy and Joseph and Leyla were here. But, Mother, you are right. The way we celebrate Christmas here is the best!" As she said this, her gaze fell and rested for a split second on the Christmas card that her aunt had sent and that was displayed in the far back corner of the altar. She quickly turned away and looked at her mother, who was smiling blissfully at her family.

"Okay, who is hungry?" Mr. Rodrigues asked.

"We are!" they all answered in unison, and they scampered out to the dining room to eat their Christmas midnight meal.

Night of Peace

Silent night, Holy night! All is calm, all is bright…
Silent Night by Joseph Mohr and Franz Gruber

That night in bed, Mrs. Rodrigues kept pondering what Isabel had told her, and then her thoughts turned to Leyla.

"There is a rare quality about the air tonight that fills one's soul with peace and love," she told her husband. "I am thinking about Leyla. Do you remember how she was always so afraid? Every little noise at night would give her such a fright—but on Christmas Eve—on a night like tonight, she could sit on the terrace of the kitchen by herself all night long. She told me that this was the only night that she felt completely safe and at peace."

"Yes. I remember her saying that," he answered, pensively, in a whisper.

"I will not be surprised if right now she is sitting outside in her garden, in the jungle of Africa, looking up at the sky and filling herself with this peace," she added. Mr. Rodrigues did not answer. They cuddled for a long time in blissful serenity.

"But what is going on with Isabel?" he finally asked. Mrs. Rodrigues told him what Isabel had whispered in her ears. He was speechless. He felt shivers run up and down his spine, and he blessed himself.

"Where does she get such ideas? I have to talk with Nhõ Padre. They have to stop telling the children all these stories. It only serves to fuel their imaginations and cause them confusion and heartache," he said, determined to have a word with the priest and the Sunday School teachers at the first opportunity.

"We all know that Isabel has a wild imagination, but I believe that something happened. Perhaps the same magic of this night that releases Leyla from her fears also has touched Isabel's heart tonight—and all of us in one way or another," she said.

"Yes, I know what you mean. Even me..." he began to admit, tentatively, something that he had not dared to admit to himself before, and now he was about to share it with his wife.

"You? What do you mean?" asked Mrs. Rodrigues, abruptly releasing herself from the bed covers, and sitting up, facing her husband.

"On this night, I am filled always with hope—hope that...that...next year the rains will come—on time—and in abundance. Hope that the harvest will be plentiful and that our storage room will be full. Hope that I will be able to buy all the children shoes and that all of them will have a chance to go to high school and even attend university in Lisbon. Hope that you will have new clothes and that I can hire someone to help you in the house so that you will not have to spend most of your time grinding corn and cooking in that smoky kitchen." Mr. Rodrigues took his wife's rough and calloused hands and kissed them and continued, "I am filled with hope that you will have the leisure time that you deserve and that your hands will be soft like those of the lady that you are, and not so calloused from constant, hard, manual work." Tears flowed down his cheeks.

She softly blotted dry his tears with her lips, saying, "It is all right. God has made us strong. He has blessed us with eight healthy and wonderful children. Hard work is nothing—the important thing is for us to provide them with a safe and happy place to grow. God will do the rest."

"Yes. On this night God fills my soul up to the brim. Just as our cereal drums are filled to the brim with corn after the harvest, my soul is also filled with hope this night. And as you dispense, throughout the year, just enough corn for our meals each day, God dispenses, each day, just enough hope to get me through. In that way we are very blessed," he said, kissing his wife's hands and bringing them close to his heart, where he let them rest.

They did not speak for a long time, and their souls swelled in heavenly peace.

Suddenly and joyfully, Mrs. Rodrigues broke the silence. "And let's not forget about the gift of Fern. It was thirteen years ago to the minute that 'n da luz (I gave light), that Fern was born. It was one of the easiest deliveries that I have ever had. Do you remember what Didi told us, after she examined Fern's placenta?" Mrs. Rodrigues reminded her husband.

"Remember? How can I forget! Didi delivered all our babies, and she always had some very good things to say about each one of our children after reading their placentas, but Fern's placenta, she said was extraordinary. Didi has practically delivered every baby in this town since she was sixteen years old, and she said she had never seen anything like that," Mr. Rodrigues added.

"What did she say about Fern conquering?" Mr. Rodrigues asked, trying to remember.

"She said that Fern would conquer the world with optimism, strength, good will, and generosity," Mrs. Rodrigues answered. They laughed heartily.

They hugged each other. Their hearts swelled up with love filling their chests, engulfing their whole bodies and each other. Their hearts kept expanding, unifying them with their household, with the people in their town and beyond the sea, until they felt one with the universe. They fell asleep praising God for the grace that had been poured out onto their family.

In their rooms Eliza and Fern were delighted with their gifts. In all their years they had never remembered such a generous display from *Nhō Bedjo*. Each put on her new sweater and modeled for the other.

"I can't wait until tomorrow to wear this. Wow! Where did *Nhō Bedjo* get these?" Fern wanted to know, "I did not see these in any stores around here."

Eliza then dabbed a drop of her perfume behind her ears. She took a deep whiff and closed her eyes, then gave a twirl around the room, "Smell this!"

Fern brought her nose close to Eliza and filled her lungs with the intoxicating aroma. She exclaimed, "This is heavenly! It will drive the boys crazy!"

"You don't think that I am going to let you use this?" Eliza responded, guarding her precious little bottle.

"Oh please, Eliza, let me use it just a bit tomorrow. Please, please. I will die if on Christmas day I smell like my old self, now that I have smelled heaven," Fern begged.

Eliza was not budging but Fern knew her and always was able to bring Eliza around on anything.

"I will trade you. One dab of your perfume for a bite of my chocolate right now." At this she began to slowly unwrap the bar of chocolate and brought it close to Eliza's nose, "Smell this! You can have a bite right this minute," she said temptingly.

Eliza considered and considered. "Okay, just one dab tomorrow."

"Okay," Fern agreed.

"One bite for one dab. I don't want you to come sneaking around perfuming yourself whenever you want," Eliza said firmly.

"Okay. One bite for one dab. I promise," Fern concurred.

Eliza immediately took a bite of the chocolate, but as soon as she did she knew that Fern would never keep to her end of the bargain. Her perfume would be the subject of many such bargains with Fern until it was all dabbed out.

The chocolate was dark, and rich with almonds. Fern also took a bite, and they both were blissfully thankful for this unusual, perhaps once-in-their-life-time Christmas. Fern kept wrapping and unwrapping the pieces of the chocolate bar, wanting to save some for tomorrow, but the pleasure that they got from munching this sweet delicacy was too much to put off for tomorrow. Tomorrow was already too far away. Finally, Fern licked the last crumbs, smoothed out the wrapper and put it on the nightstand as a souvenir. They snuggled up to sleep, but not before Fern reminded Eliza, "You took three bites, so I have three dabs of your perfume to use on very, very special occasions."

"Go to sleep, Fern," answered Eliza, in an already sleepy voice. After a few moments Eliza added, "Four dabs. It is your birthday!"

In elation Fern responded, "Thank you! Thank you!"

"Yeah! Yeah! Good night, Fern, and sweet dreams," Eliza said.

"Good night, Eliza, and sweet dreams to you, too," Fern responded.

Isabel, Ida, and Mandy were all in bed. Ida was very happy with her baby doll dressed in a soft yellow outfit. It was exactly what she had asked Santa for. She had seen it in a store window and had described it to her mother, and that was what she had asked of *Nhō Bedjo*. She promptly named the doll Daisy, and she went to bed tired out but happy, snuggling her doll. The balloon and the lollipop were extras and she would have been happy with just the doll. She laid her balloon and lollipop on the nightstand by the lamp, ready for tomorrow, to enjoy and display to her friends in the afternoon in the park.

Mandy usually asked for whatever Ida asked for, so she received also a small baby doll. Her doll was dressed in pink. She had trouble naming her doll. She asked for suggestions for the name, but none of the suggestions seemed to be of her liking.

They had all been in bed for a while when Mandy startled her sisters by yelling out, "I know what the name of my doll is. It is Maggie!"

"Good, Mandy. That is a good name," Isabel replied.

Mandy immediately started to acquaint her doll with the house and she began a litany of warnings, "Maggie, I have to tell you about the dog that lives in the yard. It likes to chew on dolls like you so be careful. Also there are some cats that also like to pretend they are hunting and if you are not careful, they may think that you are some wild animal and they might go after you. You should be careful not to cross the street because of the mules and the horses, and…"

"Enough, Mandy! Go to sleep!" Isabel called out to Mandy, rather annoyed.

Mandy kept on with her monologue with Maggie out of earshot of Isabel, continuing to tell Maggie about this and that, about how not to go anywhere unless she was with her and, and…until she fell asleep.

Isabel was restless. She was ambivalent. She was happy with her gifts and the fact that she did not get her shoes did not bother her. In her heart she had given the shoes away, and in a way she felt free, even relieved. She was grateful for what *Nhō Bedjo* had brought her, and yet she felt something nibbling at her heart. She was unsatisfied with how Christmas was turning out, and yet she knew she shouldn't be feeling that way.

The sight of the Christmas card at the altar had sabotaged her heart, and it began to knot and become small and hard just as she had felt when she had first seen Dee's Lisbon-leather shoes. It wasn't the shoes; it was something else. Was it what was promised in the card that she often had daydreamed about? She prayed to the Infant Jesus to relieve her, but it was no use. She began to consider. She got up from the bed and lay down again. She sat up. She considered some more. She saw Mandy with her lollipop halfway in her mouth, drooling. She took it out and rested it in the wrapper on the dresser. She went back to her bed and snuggled against Ida, and then suddenly she jumped up and scrambled to the next room, to the altar. Like a thief she grabbed the card and tucked it into her waistband, secured by the elastic of her underpants. Isabel was in turmoil. Her heart was pumping like it had never done before. Slowly it gave way to a soothing rhythm; her thoughts began to settle on the contents of the Christmas card. As she dozed off to sleep, she began again to see the sparkling lights on the tree, the enchanting gifts and herself peeking from the doorway.

Angel Maria

...the angel of the Lord appeared to Joseph in a
dream...

Matthew 2:13

The sky was velvety black, clear with layers upon layers
of stars. It was as though one was at the surface of the
ocean in a boat looking down into the depths, but instead
one was looking up into infinity. A sea breeze swayed the
branches of the rubber trees that lined the avenue. A cluster
of wispy clouds hung from the firmament and brought in
the visitor.

The house was quiet. Everyone was asleep. It was dark,
except for a tiny light that came from the kerosene lamp
that stood in a corner and was kept on all night long at its
lowest setting.

Isabel heard a voice calling her in a whisper. "Isabel!
Isabel! We need to get on our way, quickly." The voice persisted for a while, repeating Isabel's name several times.
Isabel woke up and rubbed her eyes. First, she thought that
it was her mother, but then she saw that it was a much
younger person resembling Maria, their household helper.

"Wake up, Isabel! I am here to help you deliver the sandals to the children. It all has to be done tonight," the sweet voice urged her.

The voice was that of a beautiful young woman dressed in a long white dress just like Isabel's little angel dress. Her face of dark skin was like Maria's, and her hair was braided into two long ropes that draped down over her breasts (just like Maria), and she sported curly bangs that spread out, opening like a flower over her forehead (just like Maria). She took Isabel's dress from the foot of her bed where Eliza had left it neatly folded, and she began to help her get dressed. Then she turned around and got Isabel's papier-mâché wings that were hanging off a hook behind the door. She walked to the dresser and got her white headband. "We have to hurry. You have to deliver your shoes tonight," as she said this she strapped Isabel's wings tightly just like Eliza and Fern had done earlier that evening and fixed the headband on her head.

"Who are you?" Isabel asked, her voice a little shaky and reluctant.

"Don't be afraid. I am an angel. Come with me. We have to fly around the world to deliver the sandals to the needy children in the world tonight."

"Where are the sandals?" Isabel asked suspiciously.

"Right here," the angel slapped her hand over her shoulder, and Isabel saw that tucked in between the angel's shoulder blades, just below the wings, was a bump, and under it there were the sandals all squished up.

They immediately flew out the window of Isabel's room. The angel's wings opened wide with such a force that the disturbance in the air shook some papayas right down from the trees. The angel's wings spanned the whole width of their house. Isabel's little wings also spread out and took life.

They rose up and up and headed down the avenue. Isabel was delighted to see her shadow passing over the rubber trees, the church, and over the house of her best friend, Dee. She giggled and looked at the angel, asking, "Where are we going, anyway?"

"We are going to the ends of the earth," the angel declared. "But first, we are going to stop at a very, very special place." Isabel thought that she saw the angel's wings flutter a little in excitement and a rare light emanate from the corners of the angel's eyes when she said, "*a very, very special place.*"

Isabel began to insist. "What special place? Where? Please tell me, Angel Maria," Isabel pleaded.

But the angel said firmly, "Shhh. Be quiet. Be still. It is in the quiet—the stillness—that you'll know." As she said this, they landed on *Cruz Grande*—the Big Cross at the eastern end of the avenue. *Cruz Grande* was a familiar lookout point where people, especially from the villa, would go to look at the ships. The lookout point was made of concrete cement in the shape of a big ship. At its bow was a big cross. The cement ship was set as if it were on a northwesterly course. The bow faced the open sea where ships disappeared and appeared on the horizon on their way to the northerly islands of *São Vicente,* and also to America. All around the inside walls of the ship were cement benches where people sat on their frequent vigils.

Isabel couldn't count how many times she had been there. It was down the avenue from her house, and often she would go there with her father or with her brother, Andy, in late afternoons. Andy used to go there a lot because, as Isabel had suspected, he was sweet on a girl who lived in one of the white houses just below *Cruz Grande.* He would stand on the bench and whistle in the wind. Isabel had learned to whistle by imitating Andy. Most everyone who went there did so to look for ships coming in or going out when loved ones were traveling, or they went there just to pass the time and to dream. Most dreamed of going to America, some day, somehow, in one of those ships.

Isabel had never been on a boat, not even to Fogo, which was practically a stone's throw from where she was standing. On clear days you could see houses as white little dots along the shores of Fogo. Only her father, her two brothers, and Leyla had ventured out to sea to other islands. Neither her mother nor any other members of her family had been given the opportunity to go anywhere. Travel was not easy and it was costly. You went on those ships only if you had some real business like going to school, as in the case of her brothers, going on business, as in case of her father or going away for good like going to Portuguese Africa, Europe or America. Wanting to travel outside Brava was in their blood. *Oh, to be traveled!*

Isabel was no exception. Like everybody else on her island, she was bitten by this traveling bug while she was still in the crib. She too craved foreign things; she too admired the *traveled ones* like her best friend Dee, who was always going to other islands and to Portugal to visit this or that relative. Isabel too dreamed about traveling, especially to America.

She even knew what type of job she was going to have in America. Isabel had it all figured out. She had heard that some people worked in different factories. Her aunt, Mana, for instance, worked in a peach packing factory in California; others worked in sewing factories. Isabel was going to work in a chocolate factory. "Imagine, eating all those chocolates every day, as much as you wanted," she would say and her eyes would glaze over with the dream.

So, while standing at the bow with the angel, with the easterly wind gently blowing at their faces, it occurred to Isabel at that moment, that since she had been *so good* during Mass earlier that evening, that the angel must have come to grant her a special wish: a glimpse at that real lit-up Christmas tree in America, just like the Christmas tree in the postcard that her aunt had sent. *Where else could be a very, very special place?* Isabel reasoned. *Yes! Angel Maria is here to grant me my special wish—a visit to a real Christmas tree with all the presents under it. I am going to America!* It was the most logical conclusion, Isabel thought, with great excitement at this realization. She was completely convinced of this.

She gazed at the sea, and she let herself be lifted up into the sky. Instead of the black, velvety mantle dotted with stars above their heads, Isabel's mind was fixed on the lights in that Christmas tree. So, with all the conviction that she could muster, she took the hands of the angel, and she let the wind fill her wings, the same wind that had filled up the sails of those old pack ships sailing to America many centuries before. She was gliding in a dream. To America, as she had seen so many ships bound for America disappearing on the far northwest horizon.

To America! To America! she shouted inside her mind, not noticing the splendor and the beauty that nature was presenting to her above her head, below and all around. Isabel had forgotten completely about the sandals and the angel's mission, and she was oblivious to the fact that they were not heading out to sea, northwesterly as ships heading to America do, but that they were hugging the coast of Brava, leaving the silhouette of the island of Fogo behind them, the distant islets on their right, and going directly to the side of the island opposite from where they had first begun.

The Boy with the Hurt Foot

...God descends to re–ascend. He comes down;
down from the heights of absolute being into time
and space, down into humanity; down further still, if
embryologists are right, to recapitulate in the womb
ancient and pre–human phases of life; down to the
very roots and sea–bed of the nature He has created.
But He goes down to come up again and bring the
whole ruined world up with him.

Miracles by C.S. Lewis

Outwardly they had been flying in total silence, but
inwardly Isabel was full of jitters and anticipation. If
the quiet was talking to her, if *the quiet* was telling her anything, she could not hear it. Its wisdom was being muffled
by the screams of excitement navigating inside her head. She
could now smell "America." America had a distinct smell;
the smell that saturated the room when they opened her
aunt's boxes from America. She could feel the glitter—she
had been transported again inside the Christmas card itself.
She touched the tree; she looked around, and nestled behind
many little packages was a big, huge package wrapped with

shiny red paper and a huge white bow. *What kind of gift would be wrapped in such a big box?* Isabel thought, and just as she was about to grab it with her two hands and peek into its contents, the angel announced softly, "We are going to *Tantum*."

The word *Tantum* jolted her back into reality with such a force that she stopped in mid-air and began to tumble down into the dark waters of the Atlantic.

"Tantum?" she screamed, completely startled by this unexpected turn of events. The loud, outraged sound sent ripples through the universe. One could say that it was so loud and so disagreeable that it reached the very ears of God—the Babe in the manger.

"Why on earth are we going there? There is nothing there but fisherfolk," Isabel demanded with forceful discontent. The angel grabbed her, with both hands.

"Yes, fisherfolk who need shoes," she answered softly, unperturbed.

Isabel had visited Tantum once with Eliza, Fern, and three of their girlfriends who had come from town to spend part of their vacation with the Rodrigues girls. One day the girls had gotten bored with the routine of Ferrero, where the family went during the sugarcane harvesting season, and begged their parents to let them explore the area a bit. Tantum was close by, just over the next ridge. Every day they saw women making their descent on a narrow trail in single file down the ridge, zigzagging down the mountain with the baskets over their heads weighed down with fish. Mr. and Mrs. Rodrigues knew most of them personally, and they would barter, sometimes fish for fresh fruit, sugar cane, cassava, sugar, oil and some *grogo*. Tantum, however, was almost a forbidden place, because there were rumors of a contagious disease that was rampant there. An illness so vile, according to some, that people would not dare even to say its name—as if by just saying the name you would put yourself at risk of catching the illness yourself.

It was taboo to mention the disease, and if they accidentally did they would immediately spit violently in the dust to break the curse.

Mr. and Mrs. Rodrigues knew better and decided to let the girls have that adventure, but they strongly advised them not to drink from any cup given to them, just in case. It was a daring adventure that the girls were looking forward to, and one that they would find themselves bragging about and recounting with embellishments over and over once they were back home.

It was a hot day, and as a sign of hospitality a woman in the fishing village had handed them a cup of cool water. It was the woman's special cup—one reserved for the rare visitor. She had disappeared inside her bungalow and appeared hurriedly blowing dust out from inside the cup. The girls, including Isabel, declined politely, but the woman persisted and persisted so at last Eliza took a quick sip, hardly touching her lips to the cup, and passed it along. The other girls followed Eliza's suit, except Andalusia. Andalusia was not about to touch the cup where everybody else's lips had been, and she came up with another way to get out of the situation without hurting the woman's feelings. She grabbed the cup and took her quick sip from the handle side of the cup, saying, "It is a thing with me. I always like to drink this way."

The woman's little boy responded immediately, "Well, that is funny. That is exactly how my father likes to drink, too!" Andalusia's face took an ashen shade, while the other girls were red-faced trying to contain their laughter.

Since then, whenever Isabel heard the word Tantum, she immediately thought of that incident.

Isabel was deep into these thoughts, when the angel began to speak again. "We are going to Tantum to visit the boy with the hurt foot."

"What boy with the hurt foot?" Isabel snapped, still not completely recovered from the shock.

The angel gently reminded Isabel of the boy that she had seen two weeks before, passing by the avenue on his way to *botica,* the health clinic, to get his foot treated. Isabel now recalled the boy. He was about her age. He was bare-foot, with a dirty cloth wrapped around the foot. The foot was infected, and his whole left leg was swollen. Maria had pointed them out to her.

"Look, Isabel, at that poor boy and his mother. They probably left Tantum *na madrugada,* in the wee hours of the morning, so that they could have a chance to see the nurse this morning. Imagine, Isabel, walking up those mountains with that foot. And that poor mother probably carried him on her back most of the way. And here you are, Isabel, pes-tering *Nhō Bedjo* for those Lisbon-made shoes while those poor souls have to walk for nearly five hours with not even a plastic sandal to protect their feet from the rocks and the thorny bushes."

Isabel remembered her unsympathetic response, "Well, it is Christmas, and Mother said that you can ask for whatever you want. Why doesn't *he* ask *Nhō Bedjo* for a pair of sandals just like I am asking for my shoes?" She remembered in pain Maria's angry and frustrated look. Now in retrospect, her heart wept for her callousness and she was grateful to God for giving her a second chance to make it right with the boy and his mother.

They approached Tantum from the sea. They could have flown over the mountains and straight across the island, and practically retracing the boy's journey to the clinic. It was the same route that her family usually took to go to Ferrero. The angel said that this way was a short cut—they had a lot do to this night.

They flew the rest of the way in silence, guided only by the wind and the celestial lights. The star–studded night lit the ocean below. The rough currents banged the waves against the rocks. Pearly white foam splashed violently against the rocks, giving the coast a wide, white, lacy skirt. A cool wind blew on their faces and filled their wings and lifted them higher and higher. Presently, without warning, there it was: a tiny light nestled among the rocks.

"Here we are," the angel announced. They immediately began to descend. The angel held Isabel's hands. The angel's wings were so expansive that Isabel practically disappeared under them.

As they approached the light, they began to see people sheltered under a grotto. At first the roar of the waves, and the enormous spray from the waves hitting the rocks, prevented them from seeing distinctly the people or hearing what they were saying. Slowly they alighted on a rock at a far corner of the grotto. The angel held Isabel up so that she could have a bird's eye view of the place. Gradually she could see a group of people. There were several little bonfires and in the center there were families huddled around listening to a woman telling a story. Isabel scanned the grotto area for the little boy with the hurt foot. She couldn't see him.

"Where are they?" she asked the angel at last.

"Look at the center near the big bonfire," the angel pointed out.

At the center there was the woman, the mother of the boy, talking. She was telling a story, and everyone was riveted. Then Isabel saw the boy reclining on his mother's bosom. His foot was still bound. The angel sat on a rock with her wings tightly folded behind her back and said, "Listen. This is the most beautiful story in the world. This is the story of when God came down to earth and became one of you. Listen carefully as all the universe is now hushed to hear this ultimate story of love."

As if by divine command, the roar of the waves became a distant hush and the spray from the waves became soft sparkles of light. All nature was quiet and attentive to the voice that was coming from the woman.

"Na quese dias…" the woman began, "In those days a decree went out from Caesar Augustus that the whole world should be enrolled. This was the first enrollment, when Quirinius was governor of Syria. So all went to be enrolled, each to his own town. And Joseph too went up from Galilee from the town of Nazareth to Judea, to the city of David that is called

Bethlehem, because he was of the house and family of David, to be enrolled with Mary, his betrothed, who was with child. While they were there, the time came for her to have her child, and she gave birth to her firstborn son. She wrapped him in swaddling clothes and laid him in a manger, because there was no room for them in the inn.

Now there were shepherds in that region living in the fields and keeping the night watch over their flock. The angel of the Lord appeared to them and the glory of the Lord shone around them, and they were struck with great fear. The angel said to them, 'Do not be afraid; for behold, I proclaim to you good news of great joy that will be for all the people. For today in the city of David a savior has been born for you who is Messiah and Lord. And this will be a sign for you; you will find an infant wrapped in swaddling clothes and lying in a manger.' And suddenly there was a multitude of the heavenly host with the angel, praising God saying: 'Glory to God in the highest, and on earth peace to those on whom his favor rests.'

Luke 2: 1–14

After she finished there was a great silence: a silence so great, so complete that it seemed that all nature was holding its breath, and all the motion of the stars and planets in the universe had stopped. The waves were frozen in place and droplets from the spray set in mid–air. Time ceased.

Finally Isabel whispered, "I have heard this story before, but, but..." Isabel struggled to explain to her companion.

The angel completed her thought, "But you never understood?"

Isabel did not reply. She immediately took two pairs of sandals from the angel, one for the boy and one for his mother, and the angel directed her where to leave them. Then the angel took a tiny pouch from near her heart and tied it to the boy's sandals.

"Angel Maria, what is that?" Isabel asked.

"It is a special gift—a fishing hook. Whenever…"

Isabel brusquely interrupted the angel, "A fishing hook?" Then she added, belittling the gift, "What kind of Christmas gift is that—he is not going to want *that* for Christmas!"

"Are you not yet to understand anything?" the angel responded, gazing intently at Isabel. Isabel was shaken by the penetrating power of the angel's gaze. Until now her eyes had not directly met the angel's. What she saw was at the same time frightfully immense and vastly beautiful and merciful. Isabel felt so small, so insignificant. All the blood from her body seemed to rush to her face. She kept her gaze away and looked toward the sea. The angel continued, however, with no judgment, "The hook is for the boy to use to fish. All kinds of fish will swarm to that hook, once he lets it touch the water. Tantum will become like it was."

"Will become like it was?" Isabel questioned.

"Yes, like it was. Like its name, 'worth so much.'" Then she added, almost as an afterthought, "If he understands and if he uses it, that is."

Isabel wanted to question the angel further about this new revelation, but the angel abruptly silenced her, "Shhh.

Be quiet. Be still. It is in the quiet—the stillness—that you'll know."

When they had flown up the ridge and the fishing village was directly below them, the angel turned around and puckered her lips and blew out. The air rushed out of the angel's lungs as in a gust of wind, but left everything still and shiny and enclosed the whole village of Tantum in a bubble. "God commanded me to leave His mark on all the people whose lives we touch this night. This fishing village is now sealed with God's protection and love."

The Old Woman and the Girl

Be still and confess that I am God.

Psalms 46:11

They sat on a rock on the mountain ridge facing the valley—Chada de Tanbarina, with Tantum now behind them. It was a *robera,* a valley that stretched out from the top of a mountain range and ran all the way to the sea. People said that this valley was once very fertile; others said no, that it was part of the sea since it was strewn with boulders of all sizes and the land was not dirt but sand. Isabel was familiar with some of the stories about this valley. This was where her family had several pieces of irrigated land in terraces along the steep mountain inclines. The family's cottage was at the foot of these mountains, and in front of the cottage was the valley with a clear view of the ocean.

While her family was in Ferrero for the sugarcane–harvesting season, every evening after supper, the sugarcane workers and other residents would join them. They would sit under the tamarind tree just outside the cottage. Usually Isabel and her brothers and sisters would sit with the town children. Every night townspeople would gather there after

supper, and they all would feast on fresh sugarcane juice—
and also the distilled—and hear the elders spin their yarns.

"This valley," an old man would reminisce, "in the time
of my great, great, great granddaddy, was a paradise." Then
there would a big pause, and he would add, "A paradise
for the pirates. They would come here from the coast of
Africa to hide from the Portuguese and the Spaniards after
marauding ships. This valley was full of tamarind trees that
produced year–round and also there were coconut trees all
along the shore. There were mango, guava, and all kinds of
fruit trees as well as wildlife. There were streams that meandered from the top of that mountain and collected in ponds
that were full of shrimp. Those pirates would come and fill
their ships with food and water. The local people would go
into hiding and take with them any livestock or anything
of value to keep the pirates from taking them. Women suffered a lot at the hands of these pirates, and men, too."

People would ask the old man all kinds of questions,
and the children trembled when he would say, "And you
children, you would have been taken to the ship like slaves
never to see your mommies and daddies again.'" He would
laugh seeing the children's reactions and continue, "Now
this valley is a desert—a wasteland—and the only sign of
piracy is that iron stake way up on that mountain top."

Isabel remembered her father's face whenever anyone
mentioned the iron stake. Mr. Rodrigues would often speak
of the iron stake on the mountaintop himself. The people
would speculate what it was for. Some would say that it
was a marker of where great pirate treasure lay hidden, but
others would say that it was only a clue. Still others would

speculate that the pirates probably used the stake to fly a flag to signal their ships. Mr. Rodrigues' eyes would glaze over dreaming about the great pirate treasure buried under his own piece of rock. They would go on for most of the night, dreaming of the times gone by, each person speculating on the meaning of the iron stake and on what kind of treasure would be found under it.

"But now," the old man would usually end his story, "there is nothing." He would get his stick, get up and spit on the ground and mumble in bitterness, "Now there is nothing but rock and sand in this valley—and this *seca*, this drought that never ends, has killed everything. The earth has become bare, and when it rains, the water drags everything out to sea."

Isabel, succumbing to the remembrance of the old man's gloom, asked, "Angel Maria, is this the end of the earth?"

The angel did not respond, but extended her right arm, pointing, and said, "Look over there!" It was very dark and the only distinguishable thing was the white foam from the roaring waves battering the rocks.

Isabel squinted, looking in the direction indicated, "Where, Angel Maria?"

The angel held Isabel closer to her, and with her right index finger drew a circle in the air. Inside the circle a hut appeared, and a minute speck of light became visible.

"Yes! Yes! I see it," Isabel said in excitement.

"Now, do you remember, Isabel?" the angel asked.

"Remember? Remember what, Angel Maria?" Isabel replied.

The angel said nothing but brought the circle even closer to Isabel's eyes. Isabel could see now a very old woman and a little girl asleep inside their hut. Isabel recognized them and remembered.

It had been one of those times in Ferrero. Isabel had been pestering her mother to let her go and visit the old woman and the girl out of pure curiosity. The old woman was a well–known local sage. What had piqued Isabel's curiosity was that people said that the wind and the sea spoke to the old woman—that she knew things that few human beings knew. The old woman hardly ever ventured outside of her hermitage. She was small and thin, spoke very little, and ate even less, they said. In one of those nightly story-telling gatherings outside the Rodrigues' cottage, someone had remarked that the old woman knew things from the voices that spoke to her in the "silence." Some said that it was the sea that spoke to her. Others said that it was the wind that howled in the night that spoke to her, but most believed that it was the silence that connected her to the very mind of God. To that, a young man had commented, "I don't know how anyone can live like that."

The old man responded, "I knew her when she was young and she always liked to be apart, and if you would ask her, she would tell you herself, 'I don't understand how anyone can live otherwise.'"

What puzzled most people was that this area was very quiet; the only noise was that from a bleat of a goat, the constant roaring of the sea far away, or the call of a bird. "The silence that she tried to explain to me once," the old man continued, "was the silence inside her head, inside her mind." People said nothing, but nodded their heads.

Isabel once had caught her mother carrying on an energetic dialogue with herself, and she asked her mother, "To whom are you talking?"

Her mother frankly told her, "No one. You know that the human mind is always active, chatting away even when it has nothing to say. It is always in turmoil, and if it does not have anyone to talk to, it invents something or someone." Isabel had understood that. She also often had caught herself talking, perhaps not out loud, but talking nevertheless inside her head about this and that. Usually it was to do with something that a girlfriend had done and how she was going to tell her off. Often she would find herself so embroiled in her inner conversation that she would not be aware of her surroundings. That earned her the title, among other things, of *pasmada* a person with the look of an empty head staring blankly into space.

Well, that day Maria had taken Isabel to visit the woman. The old woman offered them popcorn which she made right in front of them. She put some black volcanic sand in an iron pot, heated it until it was very hot, then poured a couple of handfuls of bright yellow corn onto it and covered it. Soon enough the kernels were exploding into fluffy white blossoms. The widow then gave a handful of the popcorn to Isabel, a few kernels to Maria, and even fewer kernels to herself, and the rest she gave to the girl. On their way back home, Isabel complained to Maria about how little of the popcorn the old woman had given her as compared to what she had given to the girl. She now recalled Maria's scolding.

"Don't you know anything, Isabel? That popcorn is the only thing that that girl will have to eat all day. You had a good breakfast, and your mother is now preparing a goat stew with steam-ground corn for supper. You have your belly filled every day—that poor girl only knows hunger pangs." Maria rolled her eyes in disbelief. Isabel remembered being very quiet fearing that Maria would be even angrier if she said anything, but she also remembered feeling slighted and even had mentioned it to her mother. Her mother had the same reaction as Maria, and that evening had sent Maria down to the old woman's hut with a *marmita,* a metal container full of stew and cornbread. After that day, every time that they were in Ferrero, she noticed Maria going to the old woman's hut with a *marmita* of food.

Even with the cool sea breeze blowing against her cheeks, Isabel felt the flush of shame; in daylight the crimson color of her shame would have been evident. She thanked God again for giving her the chance to make it right with the old woman and the girl.

They glided down easily from the mountain ridge, and they landed softly in front of the gate that led into the *quintal,* the courtyard. The courtyard linked the kitchen hut to the main hut. The angel lifted the gate latch and guided Isabel in. There were a couple of nanny goats tethered, a few chickens on their perch, and a dog. The angel opened her arms wide and the animals were immediately silenced.

As they were slipping inside the main hut, the scent of dried, salted fish greeted them. Isabel had not been inside the house before; in her last visit she had sat in the kitchen area with Maria, the old woman and the girl.

The main house was one big room, with a dirt floor, mud walls and a thatched roof. The walls were papered with old newspapers. A curtain of seashells sheltered the old woman's bed from the girl's bed of straw in the other corner; on a little table was a lit *lupeta*—a small lamp—fashioned from scraps of sardine cans with a rag twisted into a wick. The table was set with three figurines, Mary, Joseph and the Baby Jesus. The figurines were laid on a bed of shells—a starfish for a star, and a conch shell that heralded the good news.

The angel handed Isabel two pairs of sandals and directed her where to leave them. Isabel carefully drew her hands under her clothing and pulled out the Christmas card that she had tucked against the elastic waist of her panties, and she added it to their display without the angel's noticing. The angel took a little pouch from under her chest and tied it to the girl's sandals, and they quietly left.

Once outside, Isabel asked, "Angel Maria, did you give her fishing hooks too?"

"No, Isabel, inside the girl's pouch are three tamarind seeds."

Isabel's natural reaction was to turn up her nose at what seemed to her as a "useless" gift, but this time she said nothing. The angel explained, "These are blessed seeds, and as soon as the girl sows them, the most beautiful tamarind trees will grow. They will spread and fill this valley, and it will become the paradise that it once was, teeming with all kinds of fruit trees, birds and animals. The water will run again plentifully into streams." Then she added, almost as an afterthought, "If she understands and sows them, that is."

With these words they immediately ascended, and then, as before, the angel turned around, puckered her lips and blew out. The air rushed out of her lungs, and a bubble enclosed the old woman and the girl's hut so it was sealed with God's protection and love.

The Journey

Listen carefully, my child, to my instructions, and attend to them with the ear of your heart.

The Rule of Benedict: Insights for the Ages by
Joan Chittister

"Now to the ends of the earth!" the angel said, almost as a command. Isabel replied, "Where is the ends of the earth?"

The angel did not answer and only said, "Shh. Be quiet! Be still! It is in the quiet that you will know."

Isabel was puzzled by the angel's reply. This was the third time that the angel had told her that, and she wondered what was the meaning of, *It is in the quiet that you will know.* She thought about the boy with the hurt foot and the girl and the old woman. Would they understand what the angel hoped that they would understand? She, herself, had not understood, did not understand the lessons and the mysteries behind the gift of the fishing hook and the tamarind seeds. She said a prayer for them that they would understand, and then she added a prayer for herself, *Baby Jesus, I would like to understand too!*

They flew in perfect silence. Without Isabel noticing, they had changed course immediately after leaving Chada de Tambarina. They were headed directly east, thus explaining the angel's sense of urgency. The angel did not want to meet the Christmas morning sun head on.

They flew with angelic speed and at celestial heights. If they had been within the earth's atmosphere, the sheer power of the angel's speed would have sounded like the most powerful jet engines. It was a good thing that Isabel was well cocooned within the angel's wings so that she was completely oblivious and untouched by the elements. The jet–engine type noise might have caused her to faint; much as she had fainted from sheer fright in the park right in front of their house. With the African colonies' outcries for independence, the Portuguese, in a show of force, had some of their fighter jets fly very low over the islands. The residents had never seen and had never heard such a thing. It had brought them to their knees in fear. Some thought that the end of the world had come, and so did Isabel. She still suffered from the humiliation of often being reminded of the incident where she had turned milky white in fright. Contrary to her family's stories, she was not the only one so affected, and she was always quick to point that out.

After leaving the girl and the old woman, Isabel was very contrite. She prayed with her heart, *Baby Jesus, on this night help me understand. I do not want to be stupid and selfish, like Maria says I am. I want to understand the meaning of the gifts. I want to understand why that story that the woman from Tantum told was the ultimate story of love, as Angel Maria said. Please, on this night, please help me, Jesus.*

The silence of the cosmos beckoned her. It was a silence without a buzz, or the constant background hum that she was used to at home. It was a silence that spoke of God, perhaps. At home there was no such silence. All moments of silence were interrupted: by a chirp of a cricket, a crow of a rooster, a bark of a dog, a meow of a cat, a cry of a child, a song of a bird, a howl of the wind, or a drop of rain falling on the hot dry cobblestones.

One day, after a heavy rainstorm, Isabel had sat in front of a big puddle of water that had formed in the street in front of her house. After such a violent storm everything became still; the sky had cleared and the sun began to dry up the earth like a warm fluffy towel. She was looking at the sun reflected in the puddle when she noticed an ant trying to cross the puddle. The ant was fighting from being dragged under the water. Isabel got a leaf and helped the ant onto it, and soon the ant was crossing safely. The ant did not make any noise that Isabel could hear, but it was affecting the calmness of the puddle. It was silently creating ripples covering the whole tiny pond. Isabel now was feeling like that ant being transported through the heavens by the angel. She was creating tiny ripples across the heavens and making no noise—at least, no noise that anyone could hear. She was aware, however, of a soft noise that only she could hear—her constant breathing. The flow of air going in and coming out of her lungs made a tiny noise that she, and only she, could hear and feel. Isabel became fascinated with this. She began to concentrate all her efforts in listening to her breath and her breath alone. After a while, her mind was becoming one with the rhythm of her breath. Her mind became calm like the little puddle.

The concentration on her breathing, high up in the heavens under the wings of the angel, had transported her to an oasis: an oasis of silence buried deep within her heart. The silence began to serenade her. She began to hear the murmurs, the overtures of love stirring in her heart. The silence began to speak to her of the wonders of God, and Isabel listened with the "ear of her heart." She heard love in faint melodies calling her. She began to lose herself, surrendering completely to the alluring call of love.

The Children & the Banana Tree

Blessed are you who are now hungry, for you will be satisfied.

Luke 6:21

"We've arrived," the angel said. Suddenly, without having noticed their descent, Isabel realized that they were now flying very low, with their feet almost touching the treetops. It was still dark, and as far as she could tell they could just be in Ferrero with no electric lights—pitch dark, except that, unlike Ferrero, or any place that she had ever been, the earth was completely covered with trees.

They landed in a small clearing, and immediately the peace with which the silence had nourished her soul so sweetly during her flight dissipated. Isabel kept turning around looking every which way, hoping to see something that she recognized. Her breath became shallow and rapid, her thoughts were all jumbled; her heart was pulsating like her mother's hands beating eggs for their Sunday omelets; droplets of sweat dotted her face. She threw her arms up and kicked the earth hard with her heel, dislodging a clump of clay from its bed. Although it was dark, the glow from the angel provided enough light for her to see her immediate surroundings. *The earth is red!* she thought, furrowing her brows. *Aha! Aha! Yes, yes, those are banana trees,* she thought, relieved to have recognized something, *but the house...the house. The house is of red stone! This looks like the place where...*Isabel couldn't place it. *That is a house made of red stones. Red stone? Red earth?* she asked herself, *I have never seen anything like this!*

It was as though she had been enveloped in a cloud of fog. There was something about this place that dared her recognition...*the red stone house and banana trees.* At last she screamed out, "Angel Maria, where are we?"

The angel, who up to now had been calmly observing Isabel, replied, "You are touching the edge of your future."

"The edge of my future?" Isabel echoed. She gazed intently at the angel searching for an explanation. She leaned against a boulder in front of a grove of banana trees, waiting for the angel's response. The angel came and sat beside her, and they faced the little house of red brick, which was only a few yards in front of them. It was a square shape with a small wooden door in the middle and two windows, one at each end. The windows had no frames. Brown sackcloths draped the windows and wagged gently in the breeze. There were a few plants potted in old cans resting against the house. The clearing surrounded the house, and then there were fields beyond planted with corn, cassava, yams, and beans. Groves of banana trees dotted the area. A narrow path meandered from the main road to the clearing and the house. Isabel and the angel sat on the boulder at the far right of the house facing directly the entrance to the clearing.

"Look!" the angel commanded. At this, Isabel turned around and saw a group of people standing in front of a truck at the entrance of the clearing. There was a black woman draped in colorful clothes and two tall black men. Next to the woman was another tiny white woman wearing a bluish garment. The white woman looked vaguely familiar to Isabel. She reminded her of her mother, perhaps. These people were talking with three children: one boy of about her sister Fern's age, another boy of Isabel's age, and a small girl of about Ida's age. The children were barefoot, dirty, and wearing clothes even more ragged than those of the boy with the hurt foot.

"What about those bananas there?" the tallest man with glasses asked the children, pointing to a bunch of bananas hanging from the tree behind Isabel and the angel. Isabel turned around and looked up to see what the man was referring to. The bunch of bananas was so big and heavy that it was beginning to bring down the tree. It had a wooden stake holding it up.

"Ah! We are saving them for Christmas," the older boy answered, and everyone gave a hearty laugh. The laughter died away, taking the group with it, leaving only Isabel and the angel sitting on the boulder.

"Who were those people? And where did they come from?" Isabel asked.

"Those are the children who live here and who are sleeping inside that house. They have no parents; they are orphans, and they live here by themselves. Those people came to help them," the angel said.

"Who was that woman who looks like my mother?" Isabel asked.

"That is you," the angel responded.

"Me! How can that be?" Isabel answered.

"Well, as I said, you are at the edge of your future. That is you in about, oh, forty years or so," the angel responded.

"What am I doing here?" Isabel asked.

"Well, you are here to help, but..." the angel began to explain.

"But, but what?" Isabel asked impatiently.

"But you don't know their hearts. You don't feel their pain. You don't embrace them as your brothers and sisters. You just listen and write things down and hope that somebody else will do something, and then you leave and you never look back, or ever think of them, or even whisper a little prayer for them. You may think that you are holy, deserving the admiration of men, but you are not working to build the Kingdom of God," the angel said.

"What? Build the Kingdom of God?" Isabel replied.

"It is not for me to tell you your future—that belongs to God. But, this I am authorized to share with you." The angel picked up Isabel and held her in her lap. She caressed her hair and kissed the top of her head and began:

"You are a great being. All human beings are great beings created by God in His image and likeness, and each one of you is unique and irreproducible. There has never been, or will ever again be another human being like you, Isabel. On earth your bodies are the temple of the Holy Spirit of God. You are all children of Light. God knew each one of you, even before you were in your mothers' wombs. You all are His creations, His children, at the same time unique and different. God delights in the uniqueness of His creations, but also He delights in the diversity of His creations. For example, some of you are short, some tall, some with white skin and some with black and others with all shades in between. Some with big black eyes and others with blue little eyes and so forth. Some come to the world poor, some come rich, some with poor health, some with good health, some will live on earth for a relatively long time, some will live in the body for only a few minutes, some very intelligent, some not, some with power, some without, some kind, and some not so kind." The angel paused and asked, "Do you understand?"

"Yes," Isabel responded plainly and continued, "some live in a big house like me and some live in a small house like this one; some have shoes and some are without shoes; some have plenty to eat and some have little to eat. Some have good mothers and fathers and some have none."

"Good. This you understand. But why?" the angel asked.

"Because this is how God created it," Isabel responded.

"That is correct, Isabel. But for what purpose?" the angel quizzed.

"That I really don't know. It seems unfair to me," she responded.

"Ah! Unfair. This is the most common answer," the angel replied. Isabel was silent. She did not have any thoughts on the subject. She had nothing more to contribute. So, she tried to listen to the silence inside her heart.

After a long pause, the angel continued, "Inside that little house there are three little children—three little children whom God loves very much. They have no moms or dads."

"How can that be?" Isabel blurted out in disbelief.

"There will be a time, and these times come quite often, when a devastating disease will hit the world, and it will spread, and it will kill many, many people," the angel said. Then she continued, "It will begin to kill men first, then women and then also children. There will be many children left abandoned, like these three over there. Many children in this land will be left orphans with no place to go, no place to lay their heads, with no one to care for them. The three children who live in that house will be okay. God has blessed them with good neighbors—their parents had this little house with this piece of land, and with the help of some good people, they have learned to grow what they need to eat, to sell and to trade. They will even go to school," the angel said.

"What are their names? How old are they?" Isabel asked.

The angel said, "You'll find out at the proper time when you come here."

"Am I one of those good people who will come to help them?" Isabel asked.

"You are looking at your future and their present. Your future and their present will collide, and you will have the opportunity, the privilege, to affect the course of their lives, as they will have the opportunity and the privilege to affect the course of your life."

"Hmm!" Isabel murmured.

"Those are not red rocks. They are blocks made with the red dirt and water. They are shaped into blocks by the hands of men, and the air and the sun dry them. You mix these things to make a new thing. Water is unique, and it has its own use. Dirt is unique, and it has its own use. The heat from the sun is unique and it has its own use. The air is unique, and it has its own use. But many times in the world, at a certain moment, all things need to give up something of themselves to create a new thing. To contribute to the creation of God's kingdom on earth—the fulfillment of God's plan. Human beings are different and unique, and they have their own individual contributions, or individual missions, but at certain moments they also need to come together and give of their unique selves to the whole. The poor give their 'poorness' so that the rich can give to them their "richness." You need to be aware of this, Isabel. You ask me if you will be one of the good ones that will come to help. You can be. Be passionate, be active, be humble, and trust God, trust Jesus with all your heart, every day and every minute of your life and in everything that you do. But above all else, don't be lukewarm in what you do, and in how you live your life. Don't stand by and take notes. Do you understand?"

"Yes," Isabel said firmly and added, "Is this what the boy with the hurt foot and the old woman and the girl needed to understand?"

"Yes. And more, as it pertains to their unique selves," the angel answered.

Isabel did not quite understand, but decided again to let the silence tell her what she needed to know.

"Now to the task at hand." The angel took Isabel by the hand, and they entered the house.

The house was but one room, with dirt walls and floors, and it was very dark, but the glow of the angel again provided enough light for Isabel to see. There were some green bananas, and a little mound of beans still in their shells in a bunch, by a corner. There was a sack with corn, a few cobs showing through the hole in the sack. There were a few aluminum pots on the back wall of the house with some blue and pink plastic bowls and a few spoons. The children were huddled together, bedded in sacks with a yellow cloth covering them. The little girl had her thumb in her mouth and was sleeping peacefully next to her older brother. Isabel left each a pair of sandals. She felt sad for a moment. At the door she looked back at the kids and said a prayer to Baby Jesus for them.

Outside, Isabel asked the angel, "You did not leave a pouch with a special gift for them as you did the other two."

The angel, pointing to the banana tree staked with the heavy bunch of bananas, said, "Remember what they said about the bananas?"

Isabel nodded her head, and said, "They saved the bananas for Christmas."

"Yes," said the angel. "The bananas are not yet ripe, but with the first light of the sun they will be perfectly ripened. They will be the sweetest and the most nutritious bananas that God has ever allowed on earth, and they will be plentiful."

"Can I taste one?" Isabel asked suddenly feeling hungry.

"No. They are forbidden to you at this time," the angel emphatically replied and continued, "The shoots from that tree will continue to produce abundantly. When the children eat the fruit, they will never feel hungry again, and they will fill their beings with joy. If they remember and understand, that is," the angel again added.

Isabel immediately said a prayer that the children would remember whatever it was that they were supposed to remember and understand.

With that they rose and hovered over the house. The angel, as before, turned around and blew over the little homestead. They immediately continued with their journey, with the North Star prominently in front of them.

Children of God

We must always see in the other human beings persons with whom we shall one day share God's joy.

Let God's light shine forth–The spiritual vision of Benedict XVI edited by Robert Moynihan

They did not speak. Isabel wondered where they were headed next, but she decided not to ask the angel since she already knew what the answer would be, *Let the silence speak!*

They flew with their feet practically touching the top of the forest canopy. They followed the course of a meandering river below, foaming and spraying as the sea in some areas, and in other areas as calm as the little puddles that formed in Isabel's front yard after a thunderstorm.

At first, right after leaving the children with the bananas, the forest vegetation was so thick and lush that no ground could be seen. Isabel was goggle–eyed, delighted to see herds of strange animals drinking by the riverbanks. The animals were so big that they dwarfed the biggest horses that she had ever seen on the island. Although it was dark, the angel lighted Isabel's vision, and she could see birds nesting in the trees, and all kinds of other animals big and small, some creeping and crawling, on the forest floor. The vision and the fragrances from the forest below filled her senses. Thoughts of paradise rippled through her consciousness, but this ecstasy was as fleeting as the sparkle from the stonecutter's ax when it hits the rocks.

Soon the river was but a meandering stream; the vegetation began to thin out; the ground was laid bare inch by inch. First there were small groves of trees here and there, then, dotting the landscape were a few trees teetering in the breeze, struggling to hold onto their dignity like old men robbed of their canes. The fragrance from the earth below slowly changed—now bringing wafts of a stench—a stench that grew stronger and stronger, crying out of human suffering. Fire simmered here and there, and smoke curled upward, extending its tentacles higher and higher up to heaven in a plea. The air was hollow and hot. Isabel could hardly breathe. Suddenly a whirlwind of dust enveloped them, and they came down. Isabel coughed violently and hid her face against the legs of the angel. The angel held her up steadfastly and kept them up above the ground on a circular platform of cloud. On this small platform they both stood, and Isabel began to survey the place.

It was a thickly populated area of small huts bound together like rotten grapes in a bunch. There were small bonfires everywhere, flaring in alert, illuminating the dark corners of the compound. Cadaverous dogs guarded entryways into the huts; cats meowed their funeral song, displaying their bony rib cages, too lethargic to chase after the rats, the roaches, and other crawling, slithering things that had claimed this human purgatory as their kingdom.

Isabel held tightly to the leg of the angel and buried her face again in the angel's skirt. She peeked and slowly turned around, trying to make sense of it; trying to recognize something, but the only image that flashed through her mind was the scariest stories of hell that she had heard from her Sunday School teachers. She felt an electric shock traveling from the soles of her feet up her spine; she was nauseated, repulsed, and she screamed out, "Angel Maria! Angel Maria!" She shouted, but her voice only came out as a desperate shriek muffled by the angel's garment.

"Do not be afraid, Isabel. God is with you. God is always with you, and wherever He sends you, go with confidence. These Acholi children are His children."

"Children? Where?" Isabel asked, turning her face around and looking throughout the camp.

"Inside those huts," the angel calmly replied.

"What are they doing there? Why? What did they do?" Isabel asked, whimpering and hiding her face again in the angel's clothes.

"They did not do anything," she said firmly.

"Why then are God's children in hell?" Isabel blurted out.

"They are hiding from those whose hearts have chased away love and have embraced hatred and envy. Look! Isabel," the angel said firmly. But Isabel buried her face even deeper into the angel's legs, whimpering.

"Look, Isabel," and with this Angel Maria gently separated Isabel from her but kept the child safely on the platform. "You will not touch this ground now, but some day you will. You must look," the angel commanded. Isabel turned around and looked where the angel was pointing.

They were now on a dusty road that appeared to be in the middle of nowhere; nevertheless, it looked liked it was a well—traveled road. The angel lifted her right arm and everything cleared up and then it was midday: the sun was up in the sky beating its full force on the land. There was a convoy of trucks filled with sacks of food moving at a slow, sluggish pace. Leading the convoy was an open—air truck filled with men dressed in dark green khakis and green berets, with rifles, monitoring the countryside around them. In the middle of this convoy, perhaps fifteen trucks down, was a jeep with the same two black men, the black woman, and the woman like Isabel's mother, whom they had seen before by the banana trees. Behind them there was another jeep with another two black men and a white man with white hair. The convoy of trucks laden with food continued for another fifteen trucks behind these jeeps, fol-lowed by another open truck with men with rifles. A few yards behind these men began another smaller convoy of several private, open—air vehicles bursting at the seams with black men, women and children in colorful garments and kerchiefs wrapped around their heads in a strange fashion. The food convoy had stopped. There were murmurs going up and down the convoy in tongues that Isabel could not understand. She had fixed her gaze on the woman like her mother. The woman had her head bent down, shielding herself from whatever was going on outside. Then the angel pointed to the very end of the convoy, perhaps thirty trucks down from where the white woman was, and said in a commanding voice, "Look!"

Isabel turned around, and a shrill scream from the bottom of her little gut exploded out causing the very particles of dust suspended in the air to sift and settle to the earth. A rocket, coming from nowhere, had hit the last truck with the men and women in royal headdresses. Pieces of metal and debris from the animals, food provisions and humans showered the sky. The charred frame of the truck was tilted in a ditch by the side of the road, immobilized. Several bodies, charred and stiffened, draped what once had been the windshield of the car. Isabel's face was puffed up. Red. Her hair was covered with dust and soot, forming small tentacles framing her round face. She held to her stomach with one hand, the other hand gripped the angel. Her body convulsing and her dress drenched in sweat, she looked up and down the convoy. She looked at the woman, her future self; she had not moved. Her face was buried in her notebook. There was no sign that she was even aware of what was going on, or if she were, she felt it was not her affair. There was an eerie calmness to her demeanor.

"What is she doing here?" Isabel asked after a while.

"She is here as before," the angel responded.

"What is she looking at on her lap?" Isabel asked.

"She is looking at nothing. She is very frightened. She is thinking that she is stupid to have come here. She is thinking, 'What am I doing here? What possessed me to leave the comfort and safety of my home to come here? For what? For what?' Her fear is paralyzing her and she is becoming blind to her calling—to her purpose," the angel said.

"Why is she becoming blind to her calling?" Isabel asked.

"Fear," the angel answered.

"Well, I don't blame her for being afraid; look where she is?" Isabel pointed out.

"It is *not where she is* that is paralyzing her with fear," the angel responded.

"Then what?" Isabel answer.

"That is for God to tell you, Isabel," the angel said softly.

"So, she is here to help the children in the huts?" Isabel probed.

"Yes. Perhaps that is what she is supposed to do," the angel replied tentatively.

"Why?" Isabel paused and then continued, "Why?" She paused again, scratching her head, and continued again, "How did the children end up in the huts?" she finally asked.

Immediately the road vanished and the angel and Isabel were back by the huts where they had first stood. So the angel began.

"Time and time again, in the history of humankind, men have arisen who think that they can be God. The way that they think that they can be God is by feeling powerful. The only way that they feel powerful is by controlling people. They want total control of people—control of their bodies, their property, their freedom, and even their minds. In many cases, the weaker they are, the more they target women and children to dominate. These are cowardly men, insecure men, evil men who take delight in torturing children, in torturing women, because they believe that these are the weakest, and they will suffer no or little reprisal from it. But God, who is all good, always brings good out of evil," the angel said and asked, "Do you understand, Isabel?"

Isabel shrugged her shoulder and said nothing.

The angel then lifted her up so that she could see the expansiveness of the camp. There were thousands upon thousands of little huts filled with children and women as far as she could see.

The angel continued, "In this land, there are thousands of children and adults who have been abducted by a group with allegiance to a very bad man who wants to be called *lord.* The children are in the huts because they had to flee their homes, because thousands more of them already have been taken away from their families, and have been made slaves; some killed and some forced to do unspeakable acts. Those trucks that you see are the meager offerings from a lukewarm world; a world that sits and waits, and a world that turns its head the other way. They say, 'This does not concern us. We have to take care of our own,' and they scoff at the idea that this is really happening when they hear the stories. This is a meager offering—a half-hearted offering. Nothing hurts our Lord more, especially on this night."

"What about my offering?" Isabel asked the angel cautiously.

"This is the thing, Isabel. God created the earth with everything good in it. God created the world and gave it His infinite abundance in everything. But He also made human beings the stewards of the earth. He gave you free will. He gave you also the key to His abundance. But you tend to hoard what you have. You tend to limit what you have and what you see. When each person begins to give, when the poor offer their 'poorness and their powerlessness,' the rich and the powerful need to respond and offer their 'richness and their powerfulness.' There are no limits. The only limits that exist are in your hearts," the angel added.

"So, what about my offering?" Isabel asked again in a whisper.

"Your sandals have multiplied in the sight of God. There are sandals here for all these children and all these women and more. And so it is with everything. Once you open your heart with the key of love, God opens the floodgates," the angel replied.

Isabel was awestruck by the angel's words. In her heart a prayer of thanksgiving sprang up, and then they began to distribute the sandals. They entered each hut and found three, four and even five children strewn on the mud floors, asleep. Their feet looked like dried up old leather with cracks in the heels. Women sat against the mud walls in a stupor while babies sucked on their dried up breasts. In the darkness of the huts, an intermittent cry disturbed the thick blanket of fear that covered the whole compound. In one hut a cross, made of cornstalks, hung on a wall, but in most there was nothing. Everyone had on them what they needed for their journey. Isabel thought about the story that she had heard about the night when God's people went to sleep in readiness to leave Egypt before the Pharaoh changed his mind.

Isabel blessed herself. She blessed herself often, prompted by her thoughts and by what was taking place before her eyes. They hopped from hut to hut with angelic speed. And suddenly the angel said, "We are finished! Everybody here has sandals." The angel then blessed Isabel with a vision, and she saw a road, as far as her eyes could see, all lit up. The angel said, "These are sandals of light and they will be like the 'Word' that will be a 'lamp unto to their feet and a light unto their path.' " Then the angel said, "There is one pair of sandals left, and that is yours, Isabel."

Isabel's heart jolted in joy, but she said nothing. She felt like she did when the teacher's assistant at her school would call her name and let her participate in the school lunch with the rest of the poor children, and when she would sit next to Tonia. These were the moments when she felt privileged and more honored than when she ever felt by the requests to recite poems and sing songs to the island's most elite visitors.

Presently, they were back where they had started. Isabel and the angel sat on the platform, now raised a little higher from the ground. They could see the whole camp. The angel took out the last pair of sandals and put them on Isabel's feet saying, "You will need these sandals for your life's journeys, as *they* will need their sandals in their journeys. These sandals will remind you of this night. They will remind you of what you've learned, what you have seen and heard. These are your spirit's shoes. Only you can see them, but not all the time. When you can't see them you will feel them in your heart, you will feel them in your memory. You will remember this night. These sandals will help you on your way; they will flash in the sunlight; glow in the moonlight; twinkle in the dark." Isabel looked at her feet and the sandals twinkled and caressed her with such love that it embraced all her being.

Then she stood up, reflecting, and asked, "Angel Maria, what special gift did you tie to these children's sandals?"

"Ah!" the angel explained, "Their gift is the gift of strength, the gift of love, the gift of understanding, and the gift of joy."

Isabel tilted her head, questioning the angel.

"These are the most important gifts, Isabel. That is all they need. That is all anyone of you on earth really needs. Although they are being oppressed, they themselves will not feel oppressed; although they will be hated, they themselves will feel only love; although they will be deprived of food; they themselves will be satisfied. Do you understand, Isabel?" As she said this, the angel looked toward the east and saw in the horizon the faint orange glow of the Christmas sun. "We must hurry," she said, and quickly stood up. They rose high above the compound and she turned around and showered the whole encampment with God's love, blessings, and protection.

God is Love

I belong to my lover and for me he yearns.

Song of Songs 7:11

The Christmas morning sun was just below the horizon, sending orange flares heralding the birth of this new day. The angel set her flight at a speed that kept the sun at that position throughout their westerly journey home. Often they turned around and the angel sang, *Gloria in excelcis Deo—Glory to God in the Highest!*

On their flight back, Isabel found again the oasis of silence inside of her, and for a while love serenaded her, but the vision of her adult self kept gnawing at her, draining the waters of the oasis. Several times she felt heavy, and drawn down, and the feeling of gloom touched her soul. Whenever this happened, she fell precipitously. Each time the angel grabbed her and brought her up. After a while thoughts of her future ruptured her peace completely. The peaceful oasis of her mind was infested with chatter of "what ifs." She cried out, "Angel Maria, what about when I grow up?"

"I don't know about when you grow up, Isabel, that is God's knowledge. Don't be afraid. I will teach you a prayer, a song, that will be indelibly written in your heart. You may not remember it all the time, but whenever you begin to feel the cold icing–up around your heart, and whenever you begin to feel the fog invading your mind, this song will serenade you and will release you and put you on the path to God."

"Please teach me, please!" Isabel pleaded.

So, the angel began. First she began to sing it very softly whispering in Isabel's ears, then slowly and with every stanza she sang louder and louder in the sweetest voice that Isabel had ever heard. Then she urged Isabel to join her. They sang and sang, gamboling up in the sky with the darkness of the old day in front of them, and in pursuit, behind them, the glorious orange glare of the new day's sun. As Isabel sang, the angel wrote the words deeply in her heart.

God of Love
Jesus, Lord of Love, on this night
Let me love myself with the love with which you created me

Let me be still so that I can hear Love
Let me be quiet for the sake of Love
Let me speak with the voice of Love

Let me understand, let me be cheerful
Let me praise you all day long.

God of Love
Jesus, Lord of Love, on this night
Let me be successful in the reality of Love

Let me be generous with the abundance of Love
Let me be honest with the truth of Love

Let me be lighthearted on the wings of Love

Let me yield, let me be gracious,
Let me praise you all day long

God of Love
Jesus, Lord of Love, on this night
Let me be rich with the wealth of Love

Let me boast in the mercy of Love
Let me succumb to the demands of Love
Let me understand the mysteries of Love

Let me accept, let me be humbled
Let me praise you all day long

God of Love
Jesus, Lord of Love, on this night
Let me eat the food of Love

Let me drink the water of Love
Let me hear with the ear of Love
Let me see with the eye of Love

Let me be thankful, let me fly
Let me praise you all day long

God of Love
Jesus, Lord of Love, on this night
Let me think with the mind of Love

Let me feel with the heart of Love
Let me speak with the voice of Love
Let me act with the will of Love

Let me pray, let me love
Let me praise you all day long.

God of Love
Jesus, Lord of Love, on this night
Let me wake up in the light of Love

Let me bathe in the stream of Love
Let me dress in the cloth of Love
Let me walk in the shoes of Love

Let me think, let me work
Let me praise you all day long

God of Love
Jesus, Lord of Love on this night
Let me write with the pen of Love

Let me cook with the fire of Love
Let me dry my clothes with the heat of Love
Let me breathe in the air of Love

Let me sing, let me dance
Let me praise you all day long

God of Love
Jesus, Lord of Love, on this night
Let me grow old in the wisdom of Love

Let me rest in the arms of Love
Let me sleep in the peace of Love
Let me dream of the land of Love

Let me heal, let me comfort
Let me praise you all day long

And…

Isabel by this time was very tired and sleepy. The angel was carrying her in her arms, and she could only whisper these words,

And,
When you call me home
Let my body burn in the furnace of love
Let me cease, and
Let my spirit dissolve into the body of Love

Their dancing and singing continued until they were floating over the islands. The winds accompanying the sun had delivered them speedily and safely back home. The angel carried her in and tucked her in the little bed, next to Ida. Isabel moaned and mumbled, "Angel Maria, I know where the ends of the earth are." The angel did not respond, but she bent over, bringing her ear close, practically touching Isabel's lips. "It is where love is not!" she whispered and with that she fell soundly asleep.

The angel smiled, kissed her on the forehead and said sweetly, "*Feliz Natal,* Merry Christmas, little one." She left the house and when she was over the house she turned around, and as she had done before, she puckered her lips and blew out. The air rushed out of her expansive lungs and a bubble enclosed Isabel's house. The angel then flew up to the top of a mountain called *Monte* and she did the same, enclosing the whole island with God's love and protection.

The easterly wind blew gently, and the papaya trees swayed, the passerine birds sang, the cocks crowed, the donkeys brayed, the church bells rang, and the angel disappeared in the morning mist.

Christmas Morning

And Mary kept all these things, reflecting on them
in her heart.

Luke 2:19

Isabel woke up with a tune in her head. She lay down still
on her back looking blankly at the ceiling. She began to
hum the tune and then she sprang up and did a jig singing, "Let me praise you all day long." She felt happy and
refreshed. She stretched out her arms and looked around
the room. Everyone was asleep. She walked to the window
and opened the wooden shutters just a crack and looked out
toward the park. It was a bright sunny morning and there
was no one about.

She looked toward the mountains, and there they
were—the three little white houses practically hanging from
the mountainside. *That is Djan de Nole—somewhere behind
those houses is where Tonia lives,* Isabel thought, *I wonder if
Tonia is awake now and if Nhō Bedjo left her anything?* Isabel
looked back in her room and saw her gifts and her sisters
fast asleep hugging their dolls. She felt sad about Tonia.

Then she heard the same tune that she had awakened with in her head coming out from downstairs.

Isabel wasted no time and began to follow the tune. The tune took her downstairs, through the corridor and to the breakfast room where she saw Maria, her family's live–in helper. At first Isabel just peeked in. Maria had set up the ironing at the far end on their breakfast table and was ironing a white dress. She was in her underwear and her hair was unbraided covering most of her shoulders; her skin was brown, and she was smiling and humming as she ironed. Isabel came in. Immediately Maria said, "Well, well. What are you doing up so early?"

Isabel rubbed her eyes and said, "That tune…."

"Did I wake you up?" Maria said.

"No. Where did you hear that tune?" Isabel asked.

"I woke up with it in my head. I can't seem to get it out of my head," Maria said.

"That is funny," Isabel answered.

"What is funny?" Maria asked.

"Well, I woke up with that same tune in my head," Isabel told her.

"We must have heard it in church or somewhere," Maria responded, now sprinkling some water on the lace of the dress to get our stubborn wrinkle.

"Whose dress is that that you are ironing?" Isabel asked.

"It's mine!" Maria responded with a wide smile. "Your mother gave it to me last night. I am going to spend the day with my folks," she added happily.

"Where do your folks live, Maria?" Isabel asked.

"I would think that after all these years of living here with you, you would know by now where I came from, Isabel. My folks live in *Djan de Nole*, up those mountains there, beyond the three little white houses that you can see from the upstairs window," she said.

"Do you know Tonia? She lives around there too!" Isabel asked.

"Which Tonia? There are lots of 'Tonias' around there," Maria answered.

"Well, this Tonia is in my class. She walks with a limp. I saw her in church last night wearing an old man's coat," Isabel said.

"Ah! I know her. I pass by her house on the way to my folks' house," Maria answered.

"Is she very poor?" Isabel asked.

"Like most of us," Maria answered, now resting her iron and looking curiously at Isabel.

"I saw her last night," Isabel repeated and then she said, "I was wondering if *Nhō Bedjo* had visited her," she said.

"Yes, I am sure, but not like he visits here, if that is what you mean?" Maria answered.

"Oh!" Isabel responded thoughtfully.

"But, *Nhō Bedjo* does visit. She probably will eat something special today," Maria said.

"Like what?" Isabel asked eagerly.

"Oh, I don't know. Perhaps her parents have been putting away a few eggs, perhaps a chicken and they will have a stew. Perhaps they have been saving a bunch of bananas which will be extra sweet," Maria said.

"Sweet bananas! I seemed to have dreamt something about sweet bananas last night," Isabel replied.

"But, Isabel, I know their family. Their family is like my family. We don't have many things, but we care about each other, we have a lot of love, and that is what makes Christmas such a wonderful day," Maria said.

"Love. Love, Mother talks about that..." she added again rubbing her eyes, and then she jumped on her feet with excitement. "Maria, I have an idea, wait," she said and scurried up the stairs to her bedroom. She was back in a flash out of breath and smiling.

"Maria, can you take this lollipop to Tonia? Tell her that it is from me. Also tell her to come by tomorrow afternoon so we can play in the park, and, and, and perhaps the next time that you go visit your folks you can take me so that I can visit her at her house!" Isabel said happily.

Maria was speechless at this new Isabel. "Of course, sweetie," and she abandoned her ironing and came close to her and gave her a hug and said, "I am sure Tonia will be happy with your gift and she will love for you to come and play."

Isabel flashed Maria a big smile.

"Now, go back to bed and rest a little bit more. I am sure your parents will not be up for a while," she said.

Isabel was feeling very, very happy, and as she was leaving the room she saw a pair of brand new Senegalese sandals lying on the windowsill right behind Maria, and she asked, "Whose sandals are those?"

"Oh! *Nhô Bedjo* left them for me! You are not the only one who is going to look dashing today!" Maria laughed.

Isabel nodded her head and started up the stairs, and as she did, she saw a tiny white feather floating on the air and it rested lightly on her shoulder. Isabel frowned and considered. The little feather seemed to trigger a vague memory of something, but she couldn't remember exactly what. She picked it up and laid it flat in the palm of her left hand. She examined it with her usual intensity and attention as she often did with the little things of nature. She slowly went up the stairs to her room and flung open the wooden shutters and the windows. She gently blew the feather out and stood there mesmerized; her eyes followed the flight of the little feather as it went up and up in the sky until it was no longer visible. Suddenly she felt warm all over and a joyful sensation came from her feet invading her whole body. She looked down and her feet were dressed in the most beautiful and sparkling sandals that she had ever seen.

She jumped up and screamed out, "Oh! Oh! How beautiful. Thank you. Thank you." Ida woke up and sat up immediately in bed. The sun's rays blinded her, and she protected her eyes with her hands. She could only see the silhouette of Isabel. Isabel rushed toward Ida, showing her the special sandals. Ida saw only Isabel's bare feet.

Mr. and Mrs. Rodrigues were awake relaxing in their bed of bliss, savoring the few moments of this delicious morning quiet, when like a thief in the night, a scream shattered the peace and, like a sword, it ripped throughout the house.

"Mother! Mother! Mother!" Ida yelled out at the top of her lungs. Mrs. Rodrigues jumped out of bed and galloped toward the children's room with Mr. Rodrigues in tow. A distraught Ida pointed to Isabel saying, "Isabel has been clapping her feet and dancing and pretending that she has sparkling sandals on."

Isabel was standing unperturbed by the window admiring her feet. As soon as her parents came in, she dashed to her mother and father and said, "Look! Look at my beautiful sandals. They sparkle in the sunlight, glow in the moonlight and twinkle in the dark!" By this time Mandy had awakened and Fern and Eliza also had come in and were standing behind their parents.

"What is going on?" Eliza demanded.

"Oh, look at my feet, Eliza. Look at my sandals. They sparkle in the sunlight, glow in the moonlight, and twinkle in the dark," Isabel responded jubilantly.

"You have no shoes on, Isabel. Stop making up stories. Just because *Nhō Bedjo* did not bring you your shoes you shouldn't be pretending all the time," Ida said, annoyed.

"I am not pretending!" Isabel protested shaking her head.

"Yes, you are," Mandy replied, touching Isabel's feet. "You have no shoes on."

"Yes, I have!" she insisted.

"No, you don't!" Ida insisted.

"Yes, I have too!" Isabel said.

"No. You don't!" Her sisters replied in unison.

"Enough! Enough of this! All of you go downstairs and wash up. I will be down in a minute," Mrs. Rodrigues told them.

Mr. Rodrigues, Fern, and Eliza returned to their rooms and to their beds, shaking their heads in disbelief at Isabel's latest fantasies. Ida and Mandy grabbed their new dolls and scampered away. Isabel followed skipping happily, holding her new kerchief in her hands, wagging it to the left and to the right as she went along. But as she exited the room, Mrs. Rodrigues thought that she saw a flash of light explode off Isabel's heels. She frowned, paused in reflection for a second, and then dismissed it, reasoning, *It must be a sun ray reflecting on some metal piece by the door.* No sooner had she thought that when she heard the hollow *clomp, clomp, clomp* of a child's shoes hitting the wooden steps. She immediately raced to the top of the stairs, just in time to see the bare sole of Isabel's right foot exposed in the air as she went down the last step and turned the corner toward the corridor that led to the breakfast room. Mrs. Rodrigues gasped. Trembling and holding onto her stomach, she went to the living room and stared at the Christmas altar. She lit a candle and knelt at the altar for a long time, breathless. She prayed and kept all these things, pondering them in her heart.

Endnotes

1   *Blessed Art Thou Among Women: Reflections on Mary in Our World Today.* Cynthia Fox (editor), Melanie DeForest, Vivette Porges, Joshua Simon, and Robert Sullivan. Macmillan Publishing Co. Inc. 1997.

2   *The Cloister* Walk by Kathleen Norris, Riverhead Books, New York 1996.

3   *Rule of Saint Benedict* by John F. Thornton, Timothy Fry, Knopf Publishing Group, 1998.

4   Hail Mary full of grace the Lord is with you. Blessed are you among women and blessed is the fruit of your womb, Jesus. Holy Mary, Mother of God, pray for us sinners, now and at the hour of our death.

5   Fear of the Lord, piety, fortitude, knowledge, understanding, counsel and wisdom (Isaiah 11:1–3) The fruits of the gifts of the Holy Spirit are: love, joy, peace, patience, kindness, generosity, faithfulness, gentleness, self–control. (Gal. 5:22–23).